FASCINATION: THE SICILIAN'S RUTHLESS MARRIAGE REVENGE

Carole Mortimer

MILLS & BOON

First published in Great Britain 2007
by Mills & Boon, an imprint of Harlequin (UK) Limited,
Large Print edition 2012
Harlequin (UK) Limited,
Eton House, 18-24 Paradise Road, Richmond, Surrey TW9 1SR

© Carole Mortimer 2007

ISBN: 978 0 263 23072 7

Harlequin (UK) policy is to use papers that are natural, renewable and recyclable products and made from wood grown in sustainable forests. The logging and manufacturing process conform to the legal environmental regulations of the country of origin.

Printed and bound in Great Britain
by CPI Antony Rowe, Chippenham, Wiltshire

Carole Mortimer was born in England, the youngest of three children. She began writing in 1978, and has now written over one hundred and fifty books for Mills and Boon®. Carole has six sons, Matthew, Joshua, Timothy, Michael, David and Peter. She says, 'I'm happily married to Peter senior; we're best friends as well as lovers, which is probably the best recipe for a successful relationship. We live in a lovely part of England.'

PROLOGUE

GONE.

It was all gone.

The money had been spent long ago. In the last year, his London apartment had gone too, plus the villa in France and his red Ferrari. All of them lost to the turn of a roulette wheel.

It was a sickness; he knew it was. But, hard as he tried, it was a sickness he didn't seem to be able to find a cure for.

Last night he had lost the one thing that he had always sworn he would never use to finance his gambling, and he had let his family down in the worst way possible.

Oh, God…!

His hands tightened on the steering wheel of the car he drove—a hire-car; he had no money left to buy one of his own. His steering was instinctive as he negotiated the hairpin bends of the mountain road that took him away from Monte Carlo, the azure blue of the Mediterranean Sea sparkling invitingly far below. It was a journey which he knew, despite his efforts to fight the urge, he would make back again this evening, when the fever became too much for him and he once again returned to the fascination of the gaming tables.

How would he ever be able to face his father and Robin, and tell them what he had done? How could he ever explain his betrayal?

He couldn't.

After all the heartache he had already caused them, he really couldn't!

And that blue sea below did look so very inviting…

Maybe he wouldn't bother to turn the wheel at the next sharp bend. Maybe that was the answer to the sickness that possessed him, like a fever in his blood, drawing him back time and time again to Lady Luck.

A lady that had completely abandoned him….

* * *

Over.

It was all over.

All her hopes and dreams meant nothing now that she knew Pierre had never loved her at all. Certainly he'd never had any intention of leaving his wife for her.

She had believed him a year ago when he'd told her he loved her, hadn't cared that he was a married man, only wanted to be with him, to be loved by him, to love him in return.

She had been so sure that the son she had borne him three months ago would be the spur he needed to leave his wife. Instead, the coward had chosen to confess all to his wife, to beg her forgiveness in order to stay at her side!

Her poor little son.

Her Marco.

She had brought shame and disgrace upon her family to bring him into the world. And it had all been for nothing. Pierre didn't love her. Last night, as she'd lain replete in his arms after their lovemaking, and had begged him to come to her and their small son, he had told her the truth—

that he had never loved her, that she had merely been a diversion, another conquest in a long list of such affairs.

Tears streaked her face as she drove along the mountain road back to Monte Carlo and the family-owned hotel there. To her child. Her small, beautiful, fatherless child.

He would be better off without her!

She had no heart left now—knew that it was broken in two, that it would never mend.

If she were no longer here, then her brother Cesare would care for Marco, would protect him from the stigma attached to his birth, would care for him as his own, safeguarding him, so that nothing and no one could ever hurt him.

Could she do this? Could she end this now?

End the pain of Pierre's rejection?

His lies had brought her to this desperation.

His utter betrayal of a love she had thought so beautiful and perfect…!

Yes, she accepted, as she looked at the Mediterranean glittering and beckoning so temptingly far beneath her, like a diamond. Yes, she could do this. She could drive off the edge of this cliff and end the pain once and for all…

He had no idea there was a car approaching from the other direction. He only had time to register that neither of them had attempted to turn the bend in the road. The two vehicles met, joining with a crunch of screeching metal, then hurtled off into nothingness.

He turned to look at the driver of the other car, to register the beauty of the young woman's face, and she looked back at him with haunted dark eyes.

And then the two vehicles began to fall, plunging down towards the deep, mesmerising depths of the Mediterranean….

CHAPTER ONE

'THE WOMAN WITH Charles Ingram—do you know who she is?' Cesare demanded harshly.

'Sorry?' Peter Sheldon, his male acquaintance, frowned his confusion.

Cesare's mouth tightened as he bit back his impatient reply. After all, despite being at a charity dinner, the two men had been in the middle of a business conversation when Cesare's attention had wandered. He'd been captivated by the woman who stood across the room at Charles Ingram's side, looking so glitteringly gorgeous.

Next to Cesare's bitterest enemy!

Cesare gave a smile, which showed the even whiteness of his teeth against his olive skin, but which did not reach the darkness of his eyes. 'I was merely wondering who the beautiful woman is accompanying Charles Ingram...' he voiced more calmly, his tone deliberately neutral even as his narrow-eyed stare remained on the ill-matched pair.

Charles Ingram was aged in his late fifties, silver-haired, and still a handsome man. In a room full of beautiful women wearing glittering jewellery and designer gowns, and elegantly suave men in tailored dinner suits, the tall, graceful woman who stood at Charles Ingram's side still managed to stand out as extraordinary.

Her hair was the colour of honey, falling in lustrous waves halfway down her spine, and her eyes, even from this distance, were, Cesare could see, a deep, deep violet. She was laughing at something Charles Ingram said to her now, those eyes glowing. Her skin was a creamy magnolia, her mouth a full, tempting pout, her neck long and smooth, and the deep swell of her breasts was visible above the simple white gown she wore that nevertheless hugged the perfection of her alluring curves.

One of her hands—slender hands that could and no doubt did caress a man to the edge of madness—rested slightly possessively on the arm of her escort, and Cesare found himself gritting his teeth at the air of intimacy, of exclusivity, that surrounded the couple, despite the vast difference in their ages.

'A beauty, isn't she?' Peter Sheldon murmured appreciatively. 'Beautiful, but unattainable,' he added regretfully.

'Ingram has exclusive rights, you mean?' Cesare questioned hardly, his jaw clenching just at the thought of all that sensual beauty being wasted on Charles Ingram.

'Not at all,' his business acquaintance dismissed humorously. 'The lady in question is Robin Ingram—Charles's daughter,' he explained dismissively, when Cesare looked at him blankly for several seconds.

Robin Ingram.

Charles Ingram's daughter?

Not the mistress Cesare had imagined at all. She wasn't a mistress whom, just as an amusement to himself, after noting her own interested gaze fixed upon him, Cesare had been happily contemplating seducing away from her aging lover.

In the last three months Cesare had gathered all the information that he could on Charles Ingram—wanted to learn everything that he could about his sworn enemy, up to and including his shirt size.

Ingram's second child had been included in that information, of course. But Cesare had assumed—erroneously, it now seemed!—that Robin was Charles Ingram's younger *son,* and as such of little real interest.

'I had thought that Robin was a man's name?' Cesare enquired. His English was faultless. As was his native Italian, and his French, German and Spanish.

'It can be,' his companion acknowledged lightly. 'But it's also one of those names that can be used by either sex.'

So Charles Ingram's second child—Robin—was a woman... A beautiful, sexually alluring woman.

Which perhaps changed the direction of Cesare's plans for his revenge on the Ingram family....

'Daddy, do you know that man? No, don't look over yet,' Robin pleaded huskily, as her father would have turned to look in the direction of her own fascinated gaze. 'There's a man across the room—a dark-eyed, foreign-looking man—'

'A *handsome,* dark-eyed, swarthy-looking man?' her father teased lightly.

'Well…yes,' she conceded with a slight grimace. 'But that isn't the reason I noticed him.'

'No?' Her father smiled indulgently.

'No,' she insisted. 'He's been staring at me for the last ten minutes or so—'

'I would stare at you too, if you weren't my daughter!' Charles assured her laughingly. 'You look exceptionally beautiful tonight, Robin,' he added approvingly as he sobered. 'I'm glad you persuaded me to come here with you this evening. You were right. We can't keep hiding away from everyone just because they might mention Simon.'

Robin dragged her eyes away from the man staring at her so intently from across the other side of this crowded and noisy room and looked at her father instead, easily recognising the lines of grief that still creased his brow and grooved beside his nose and mouth.

The last three months hadn't been easy for either of them—the unexpected death of her brother Simon in a car accident having ripped their lives apart.

It was a loss that neither of them had come to terms with yet, and perhaps they never would completely. But she had persuaded her father to come to this charity dinner with her this eve-ning—had felt that it was time they picked up the threads of their lives again, and that it was what Simon would have wanted.

'Anyway, let's forget about that for now and get back to your handsome dark-eyed stranger.' Her father deliberately infused jollity into his tone. 'Which one is he?' He turned to look across the room crowded with socialites who had paid five thousand pounds a head to attend this event this evening.

'You can't miss him,' Robin replied ruefully, as she once again found herself the focus of eyes so dark that they appeared almost black. 'Tall. Very tall,' she amended as she realised the man stood several inches above most of the other men in the room. 'Probably aged in his late thirties. With slightly overlong dark hair,' she elaborated, affected by his glittering dark eyes. In spite of herself, a shiver of awareness ran the length of her spine. 'He's standing next to Peter Sheldon— what is it, Daddy?' She turned to to her parent anxiously as she felt the way Charles's arm suddenly tensed beneath her fingers.

'I want you to stay well away from him, Robin!' her father advised abruptly, and he deliberately moved so that he was standing protectively in front of her, rather than at her side.

'But who is he?' Robin stared up at her father, slightly taken aback by the grimness of his expression.

'His name is Cesare Gambrelli,' Charles bit out tensely.

Gambrelli… Why did that name sound so familiar to her?

Only the name, of course; if she had ever seen or met this man before Robin knew she would definitely have remembered him!

'Italian, obviously,' her father continued to explain. 'Mega, mega-rich. Amongst other things, the owner of the Gambrelli hotel chain.'

That must be why his name sounded so familiar. Of course Robin knew of the exclusive Gambrelli hotels. She had even stayed in several of them on occasion.

But who *didn't* know of the luxurious, exclusive establishments that graced most of the capital cities in the world? Or of the Gambrelli media consortium, the music and film studios, the Gambrelli airline?

And this man, Cesare Gambrelli, the man who had been staring at her so intently, was the owner of all of them…

Although that didn't explain her father's obvious aversion to him.

'I don't understand,' she said, puzzled. 'What— Don't look now, Daddy,' she exclaimed in a low voice, 'but I think he's coming over!'

At five feet ten inches tall, in her three-inch heeled white strappy sandals, Robin could quite easily see over her father's shoulder that Cesare Gambrelli was making his way deliberately across the room towards them.

'Charles,' Cesare greeted the older man emotionlessly as he moved to stand between father and daughter, making no effort to offer the older man his hand before turning to look at Robin Ingram with narrowed dark eyes. 'And I believe this is your beautiful daughter…?' he enquired smoothly.

'This is Robin, yes.' Charles Ingram was obviously rattled by his sudden appearance. 'I'm surprised to see you at an event like this one, Gambrelli.'

Cesare ran his vision slowly over the flawless features of Robin Ingram—the sensual pout of the fullness of her mouth was seductive, and those violet-coloured eyes were as beautifully alluring, the creamy swell of her breasts as full and tempting, as he had imagined! Then he slowly returned his attention to the older man. 'You think me an uncharitable man, Charles?' he challenged.

Robin had sensed already what her father thought of this man, and that impression was enhanced after only a couple of minutes in his company—he was dangerous!

A tall, dark, deadly predator!

And the most handsome man she had ever set eyes on. His eyes were so dark they appeared black, his nose was aquiline, his sculptured lips hard and unyielding, his chin square and determined, and his hair, as dark as ebony, was brushed back from his brow to rest silkily on the white collar of his evening shirt. His shoulders were wide and muscled, his body lithe and powerful. But he was also, without a doubt, the most dangerous looking man Robin had ever seen!

The way he had looked at her just now—those dark eyes had dissected every creamy curve of her face before lingering slightly suggestively on the warm swell of her breasts above the strapless white dress she wore—had only succeeded in deepening her awareness of him.

In fact, she could still feel the slight flush to her cheeks, and her breathing was uneven. Caused not by embarrassment or awkwardness in his company, but by the sharp, stinging sexual awareness which hardened her nipples and encouraged a moist heat between her thighs!

'Not at all.' Her father was answering Cesare dismissively. 'But this dinner is in aid of a British charity—and charity begins at home, doesn't it?'

That sculptured mouth tightened slightly. 'So the saying goes,' Cesare Gambrelli acknowledged softly. 'But you are wrong concerning my nationality, Charles,' he added. 'I am Sicilian, not Italian.'

Robin was aware of her father swallowing hard as Cesare Gambrelli silkily supplied this information, at the same time realising there was an increase in her father's tension at the challenge that could clearly be heard in the other man's honey-coated voice.

What was going on here? Because it was clear to her that something other than surface conversation was simmering between these two men.

There was a friction, a double meaning to their exchange, that implied they weren't talking about this charity dinner at all, but something much deeper…

'My mistake,' her father murmured in reply to the other man's comment.

A costly one, as far as Cesare was concerned. Sicilian men were not known for their forgiveness. As Cesare did not forgive the Ingram family for taking his sister from him—for taking Marco's mother from him.

'You are enjoying the evening so far, Miss Ingram?' Cesare deliberately turned his full attention on Robin, knowing by the way her breasts had tautened and hardened against the soft material of her gown, their quick rise and fall as she breathed, that although she was aware of the tension between her father and himself, she was also sexually aware of him.

Good, Cesare noted with inner satisfaction.

He hadn't completely rethought his plans yet, but he already knew that his plans for revenge were no longer set so rigidly on Charles Ingram. The beautiful Robin Ingram offered a much more enjoyable form of revenge than her father ever could.

'Yes—thank you,' she answered huskily, and she lowered long dark lashes over her violet-coloured eyes.

Modestly. Shyly. Almost coyly. And yet Cesare already knew that Robin Ingram was none of those things.

Peter Sheldon, once prompted, had been quite knowledgeable about Robin.

She was twenty-seven—ten years younger than Cesare—but she had been previously married for three years, to a knight's son, no less, although there were no children from the union. She had returned to using the name Ingram after her divorce a year ago, and had shown no inclination since to repeat the experience—hence Peter's re-mark that she was 'beautiful but unnattainable'.

Enough of a challenge to any red-blooded man, but even more so to one so bent on revenge as Cesare.

'My friend Peter Sheldon tells me that you were involved in the organisation of tonight's event, Miss Ingram,' Cesare drawled evenly. 'You are to be congratulated.' He gave an abrupt inclination of his head.

'Thank you,' she repeated. 'But as we haven't even eaten yet your congratulations may be a lit-tle premature,' she added with a tinkling laugh.

Cesare regarded her consideringly. It had irri-tated him slightly to learn of her marriage and divorce, although he accepted that at twenty-seven she was hardly likely to still be a virgin. Nevertheless, he was interested to know who had divorced who, and for what reason…

'Unfortunately I will not be staying for the meal,' he told her politely, inwardly pleased when her face registered surprise. 'I have…personal

commitments that require me to be elsewhere,'
he explained softly.

'Really?' Her voice had sharpened slightly.

Cesare held back a smile as he heard her dis-
pleasure at the obvious—and mistaken—as-
sumption she had made about those 'personal
commitments'.

'Yes, really,' he confirmed mockingly. 'But I
trust that the rest of the evening will be as successful for you.'

'I hope so too,' Robin answered him, annoyed
with herself for the way her imagination had
gone into overdrive at the mention of Cesare
Gambrelli's personal commitments that required
him to be elsewhere.

Though it wasn't too difficult to imagine what
those personal commitments might be.

And it could be of absolutely no interest to her
if he was off to spend the rest of the night in bed
with a lady-friend!

Could it…?

She hadn't so much as had dinner with a man
since her divorce a year ago, let alone felt herself

sexually aroused just looking at one! Yet she was still aware of that tingling in her breasts, of the slight dampness between her thighs, of her heightened sexual awareness that made her conscious of every single thing about Cesare Gambrelli.

A man her father had very firmly warned her to stay away from…

'I believe it's time for us to go into the banquet,' she said, noticing with relief the three hundred or so guests beginning to make their way through to the room where they were to eat and be entertained. 'It was nice to meet you, Mr Gambrelli,' she added—for graciousness' sake, rather than out of any real sincerity.

This man unnerved her. His dark good looks unnerved her. The way he stared at her so intently with those glittering black eyes unnerved her.

Her father's obvious wariness of Cesare Gambrelli, despite his own success as a wealthy businessman, unnerved her even more!

'Was it?' Cesare Gambrelli came back dryly, and his hard mouth curved derisively as he continued to look at her intently. 'In that case, I must ensure that we meet again, Robin. *Soon,*' he emphasised.

Robin swallowed hard, her throat moving convulsively, a nerve pulsing at its base. A movement closely watched by Cesare Gambrelli before he raised hooded lids to once again hold her gaze disconcertingly.

'Very soon,' he added softly, before nodding abruptly to her father and striding away on long, powerful legs.

'I want you to stay away from that man, Robin,' her father repeated emphatically, a slight pallor beneath his skin.

'But why—'

'Just trust me on this, Robin,' her father interrupted, 'and please just stay away from him. The man is dangerous. I can't emphasise that to you strongly enough!'

Echoing the thoughts Robin had about Cesare Gambrelli only minutes ago!

And after the way Cesare had made her feel, with her body still thrumming with need, Robin had every intention of keeping away!

Although she had a feeling, after Cesare Gambrelli's last comment—promise?—that he had every intention of doing exactly the opposite....

CHAPTER TWO

'IT IS GOOD of you to receive me, Miss Ingram,' Cesare Gambrelli murmured, and Robin rose gracefully to her feet as he was shown into the sitting room of her father's London home.

Had she had a choice?

She didn't think so!

The man had come to the door and asked to see her father, only to be told that her father was out but that Robin was at home. At which time Cesare Gambrelli had asked to see her instead.

Despite her father's warnings—which, though she had urged him, he had adamantly refused to give a reason for—it would have appeared churlish, if not downright rude on her part, to have refused to see Cesare Gambrelli when he had already been told she was present.

So, not exactly a choice on her part, was it?

He looked just as tall and arrogant as he had when they'd met six days ago, although today he was dressed in a dark business suit and a pale blue shirt, with a navy blue tie neatly knotted at this throat, rather than the formal evening clothes of their last meeting.

After his final comment to her at the charity dinner—the promise in his voice—Robin had known she would see him again, of course. She just hadn't known when or where. Certainly she hadn't expected that he would actually come to her father's city house, into which she had moved back since her separation and divorce.

'Won't you sit down, Mr Gambrelli...' she invited and she indicated one of the sumptuous armchairs that matched the sofa she had been reclining on, reading a book, before his arrival.

'Thank you,' Cesare accepted.

Robin had made the suggestion as a way of perhaps lessening the nerve-tingling effect of his powerful presence on her. He seemed to dwarf the spacious room. But even as he sat down, she knew it hadn't worked; she was still just as aware of him—could feel the flush in her cheeks and the way her nipples had hardened beneath the cream silk blouse she wore with casual black trousers.

Perhaps it was the way he was looking at her with those dark brown eyes, from beneath hooded lids—as if he were stripping each piece of clothing from her body to reveal the creamy curves beneath.

Whatever the reason, she was just as aroused by this man as she had been a week ago—could almost feel those long hands caressing her, the feel of his lips against her flesh as he tasted her...

She sat down on the edge of the sofa, lacing her slightly trembling hands together to look across at him enquiringly. 'What can I do for you, Mr Gambrelli?'

Many things, Cesare acknowledged to himself as he regarded her, a knowing smile curving his lips.

This woman, whose beauty was no less striking today, with that honey-coloured hair loose about her shoulders, had the sort of body that could give a man so much pleasure she would have the ability to drive him completely out of his mind.

Not Cesare, of course. Any relationship *he* had with this woman would be of his choosing, his design, his control.

A nerve pulsed in his jaw and his mouth tightened before he answered her. 'Perhaps we could start by having you call me Cesare…?' he invited smoothly, and he saw the flush deepen in her cheeks.

Not the blush of a maiden—at twenty-seven, having been married and divorced, she certainly wasn't that! But the heated colour of sexual arousal. Her eyes had become almost purple with the depth of her response.

He could see her breasts through the sheer material of her blouse, through the cream outline of her bra, their dark, aroused tips clearly visible through those thin layers of silky fabric as they pouted invitingly.

Though she looked almost prim and proper, sitting on the edge of the sofa, her hands modestly linked, her knees pressed together, as Cesare's gaze moved slowly down over those aroused breasts to her slender waist and below, he knew without a doubt that she wasn't sitting like that out of modesty—that she would be moist between her thighs as her body readied itself with the sexual desire she was unable to hide from him.

Robin Ingram—the unattainable Robin Ingram—wanted him with a fierceness she couldn't hide!

Which should make the next few minutes much simpler for both of them.

This was awful, Robin decided, and she shifted uncomfortably on the sofa, very aware of the heat of her body just from looking at this man.

Damn it, if he ever stripped off in front of her, revealing that dark, muscled body in all its naked glory, she would probably have an orgasm right then and there!

'Very well…Cesare,' she accepted tautly, forcing her gaze to meet his. 'I believe you wanted to see my father?'

'No,' he came back dismissively. 'It was always my intention to call on you.'

Robin blinked, frowning slightly. 'But I thought you asked to see my father…'

He gave a terse inclination of his head. 'In the knowledge that he was not here.'

Robin stared at him, no longer sure what was going on. If Cesare had known her father was away from home when he called, then why had he bothered to ask?

'I don't understand.' She gave a puzzled shake of her head.

'No,' he accepted dryly. 'But I can assure you that you very soon will.'

The threat in his tone was unmistakeable now, causing a shiver of apprehension down Robin's spine.

She stood up abruptly, her cheeks warm with anger now. 'I don't know what game it is that you're playing, Mr Gambrelli, but I can assure you—'

'No game, Robin,' he cut in, dark eyes glittering as he looked up at her, his expression scornful, his jaw clenched. 'Sit down,' he instructed coldly.

'How dare you—'

'I said sit down, Robin,' he repeated.

'Must I remind you that you're a guest in my home, Mr Gambrelli? An unwelcome guest at that!' she snapped. 'And that I don't take orders from anyone!' she added furiously.

'You will sit down,' Cesare told her calmly once again. 'The two of us will talk. Or rather, I will talk, and you will listen,' he amended. 'And when your father returns home later this afternoon you will inform him that you have decided to become my wife.'

'Your—your—' Robin stuttered in stupefied outrage. 'I most certainly will not!' she scorned incredulously. 'Are you taking medication, Mr Gambrelli?' she exclaimed. 'Would you like me to call you a doctor?'

'I am not taking anything, Robin,' he assured her with icy calm. 'Neither am I insane,' he added, as he saw the wary way she was now looking at him.

With not a trace of sexual arousal left in

her tensed-for-flight body, he noted with hard amusement.

No matter. There would be plenty of time for that once she was his wife. He envisaged a lifetime of exploring the delights of this woman's body.

Once she had married him…

He had made a more thorough investigation of Robin Ingram—briefly Mrs Robin Bennet—during the last six days, and now he even knew exactly what her bra size was, amongst other things that she would probably rather he nor anyone else didn't know about her.

Cesare's mouth tightened as he thought of her failed first marriage, of the real reason her husband had divorced her. And it had nothing to do with the 'incompatibility' that had been quoted on the petition.

Many things would change for Robin once she was his wife. She would become Marco's mother, of course. But Cesare also intended her to bear him more sons and daughters. He intended for the beautiful, the accomplished, the elusive Ms

Ingram to become Mrs Cesare Gambrelli, and to spend at least the next few years barefoot and pregnant!

Suitable retribution, Cesare believed, for this woman's brother taking the life of his own sister, Carla—for depriving Marco of his mother.

Although he very much doubted that Robin was going to see it the same way he did.

Not that it mattered what her objections were. He had other inducements, to bend her to his will—if necessary. And, from the look of rebellion on her exquisite face, it seemed as if that was going to be the case.

Again, it did not matter. He would not be thwarted in this. Robin Ingram would become his wife, and Marco's mother, whether she wanted to or not.

'Sit down before you fall down!' he ordered.

Was her apprehension—her fear of this man— so obvious? Robin wondered with an inward wince.

Well, of course it was! What woman wouldn't be nervous in the company of a man—a man she barely knew—who had come into her home and arrogantly informed her she was to be his wife?

'I would rather stand, thank you,' she informed him with dignity. 'And I really would like you to leave now,' she added firmly. 'You're obviously suffering under some delusion that I wish to marry you, and—'

'Let me assure you that I am not suffering under any delusions at all where you are concerned, Robin,' he informed her with a hard, humourless laugh. 'You are the spoilt, pampered, overindulged daughter of a man who had absolutely no control over either of his children—'

'Would you please leave!' Robin cut in forcefully, trembling.

'—and you are the sister of the man responsible for killing *my* young sister!' Cesare Gambrelli continued harshly, as if she had never spoken.

Robin stared at him, her eyes deep purple smudges in a face gone suddenly white.

Gambrelli...!

She had thought the name sounded familiar a week ago, but once her father had explained he was the multi-millionaire Cesare Gambrelli she had reasoned that must be why she recognised it.

But now she remembered.

Now she knew!

Her brother Simon's car had collided with another vehicle when he had been so tragically killed in Monaco three months ago. And the driver of that other vehicle, who had also died, had been a young woman called Carla Gambrelli.

Cesare Gambrelli's sister…?

It had been a very traumatic time for all of them. But she was sure, once her father had recovered sufficiently, he had sent a letter of condolence to Carla Gambrelli's family. To Cesare Gambrelli…?

She shook her head. 'As my father wrote at the time, we're so very sorry for your loss, Mr Gambrelli—as we are for my brother's—'

'I do not want your apologies!' he rasped forcefully, and he surged to his feet, once again dominating the room with his powerful presence as he glared at Robin with fiercely black eyes. 'No amount of apologies can bring my sister back to me,' he grated.

'Or my brother Simon,' she reminded him quietly, her chin raised in challenge.

Her father had never mentioned whether or not he had received any acknowledgement of his note—although from Cesare Gambrelli's behaviour now, she somehow doubted it!

Cesare gave a scornful snort. 'Your brother was a wastrel and a gambler. A man without honour. A man who was no loss to anyone. Whereas—'

'How can you say that?' Robin gasped incredulously.

'I say it because it is true,' he told her, every inch the arrogant Sicilian that he was. 'Your brother had lost everything to his gambling habit; he was a disgrace to his family—'

'I believe that is for my father and I to decide,' Robin interrupted emotionally. 'Look, I realise that you're upset about the death of your sister, Mr Gambrelli. And I can sympathise with that—really I can. But your sister and Simon collided on a steep and winding mountain road. No one knows who was responsible. You can't seriously place the blame for your sister's death on Simon—'

'I can and I do!' he assured her fiercely, once again filled with the frigid rage he had felt on hearing how his sister had met her death.

For so long it had just been the two of them—Cesare and Carla—their mother having died when Carla was born and Cesare was only eleven years old. The bringing up of his baby sister had been left to Cesare as his father took to drink, which had eventually killed him when Cesare was twenty-two and Carla eleven.

Cesare had loved his sister dearly, had cared and protected her all her life—and Simon Ingram had killed her!

'Your brother had been at the casino the whole of the evening before the accident occurred,' he continued disgustedly. 'Several witnesses have confirmed that he was extremely upset by his losses, that he was belligerent and aggressive, and that he got into a fight with one of the other patrons before he left the casino,' Cesare sneered scathingly. 'Whereas Carla had been to dinner with friends in Nice that night—I have spoken to Pierre and Charisse Dupont, and they both confirmed that Carla was happy and cheerful when she left them. My sister was a careful driver, Robin—of the two, which do you think more likely to have caused the accident?' he finished.

If anything, Robin Ingram looked even more beautiful with her face so deathly pale, her deeply violet eyes huge in that pallor, the fullness of her mouth trembling slightly.

She gave a shake of her head, her honey-coloured hair moving silkily across the narrowness of her shoulders and the fullness of her breasts. 'The police report was totally inconclusive as to the cause of the accident—'

'I know what the police report said, Robin—I asked which of the two *you* think was responsible,' Cesare cut in forcefully, black eyes gleaming.

Robin looked away from his accusing gaze, shaking slightly, not knowing quite how to answer him.

Both she and her father had been aware of Simon's gambling habit. Of the fact that he'd become aggressive and upset when he lost. Which had been most of the time.

But for this man to imply—

No, he hadn't implied anything—he had clearly stated that he held Simon responsible for his sister's death.

But that still didn't explain how Cesare Gambrelli jumped from that accusation to demanding that she marry him!

She straightened her shoulders, lifting her chin as she once again met that angry black gaze. 'The accident was a tragedy for both our families, Mr Gambrelli.' She spoke softly. 'I don't believe that either of us attaching any sort of blame as to its cause is going to help the situation. It certainly won't bring my brother or your sister back to us!'

'Or Marco's mother,' Cesare Gambrelli put in.

Robin hesitated. This conversation had become surreal several minutes ago, but now she had definitely lost the plot!

'Marco…?' she repeated.

His mouth twisted humourlessly. 'Something else you have chosen not to acknowledge? Or did you seriously not know?' he added scathingly, his dark eyes narrowed on her pityingly now.

'Know what?' she echoed dazedly.

'That at the time of her death Carla was the mother of a three-month-old baby boy!' Cesare declared.

Robin's knees buckled slightly as nausea washed over her, and she staggered back slightly to drop down onto the sofa.

Carla Gambrelli had been a *mother* when she'd died so prematurely?

Her death had left a three-month-old baby motherless?

Robin swallowed hard, trying to fight down the nausea. Losing Simon had been traumatic—a tragedy neither she nor her father would ever get over. But Cesare Gambrelli's loss was just too awful to contemplate...

She looked up sharply. 'Where is the baby—your nephew—now?'

Cesare Gambrelli looked down his haughty

nose at her, with no sign of softening in his expression at her obvious shock at what he had just told her. 'Marco is with me, of course,' he replied.

'But I… What of his father?' Robin prompted.

'There is no father.'

Well, of course there was a father. There had to be a father! Even if, as Cesare Gambrelli's manner indicated, he perhaps refused to acknowledge his son…?

Which, considering Carla's brother was Cesare Gambrelli, was either very brave or very stupid of him!

'There is no one but me,' Cesare Gambrelli informed her tersely. 'Which is why Marco is now my adopted son. A son who needs a mother,' he concluded pointedly.

Robin gave a pained frown. Was this the reason? Was Marco the reason this man was demanding that she marry him? So that she could act as replacement mother for Marco, because Cesare believed her brother, Simon, had taken Carla away from him?

It was ridiculous.

Insane.

Cesare Gambrelli couldn't seriously think she would ever—

He did, she realised, as she looked up into his hard, uncompromising face.

She shook her head. 'I'm sorry. I really had no idea. But it still doesn't change the fact that your marriage proposal is a preposterous idea—'

'It was not a marriage *proposal,* Robin, but a statement of intent,' Cesare told her, totally unmoved. 'You will become my wife as soon as the arrangements can be made.'

'You can't force me to marry you, Mr Gambrelli,' she came back defiantly.

'I thought we had agreed that you would call me Cesare,' he reminded her.

'You decided that!' Robin corrected. 'And no amount of bullying on your part is going to make me marry you!' she added determinedly.

Cesare remained impervious to her claim, seeing the two wings of angry colour in her cheeks as she looked across at him.

'Is it not?' Cesare's voice was velvety soft. 'Oh, but I think it will, Robin,' he assured her.

She looked up at him uncertainly, her gaze searching the complete implacability of his expression.

His original plan of retribution on the Ingram family had not involved marriage, Cesare admitted, but since meeting Robin almost a week ago he had decided that this was a much more practical solution. Marco would once again have the mother he was so desperately in need of, rather than the nanny who cared for him now. A mother who, as Cesare's wife, would also provide *him* with suitable entertainment.

Entertainment Robin Ingram had not seemed to view as so unpalatable a short time ago…

'Come, Robin,' he bit out impatiently. 'Sharing my bed would not be so…unacceptable, would it?'

Sharing his bed. Robin's panic-stricken thoughts echoed his words desperately.

Minutes ago she'd had only to look at this man to know she wanted him in a way she could never remember feeling before. But it was a desire that had completely deserted her once he'd told her that he intended marrying her out of misplaced revenge!

She had already escaped one marriage, which had been so disastrous she had no desire ever to repeat the experience. Had spent the last year totally avoiding even dating, let alone becoming seriously involved with anyone, knowing she had earned herself the reputation of being frigid and aloof.

Something Cesare Gambrelli's overt sexuality didn't even allow for!

She didn't need to know any more about him to realise that a marriage between herself and Cesare Gambrelli would be even worse than the disaster of her first marriage!

She gave a firm shake of her head. 'That question doesn't even merit an answer— What are you doing?' she gasped as Cesare Gambrelli reached her side in one forceful stride to pull her to her feet and straight into his arms.

'Well, if you do not know, Robin, then perhaps

I had better show you!' he came back mockingly, before his head lowered and his mouth claimed hers.

She was too surprised initially either to fight or respond to the sudden onslaught—was aware only of a leaping of her pulse rate, of the way her hands moved up to grasp the broadness of his shoulders in order to stop herself falling, of how strong and muscled they were, as was the rest of his leanly hard body as he pulled her in tight against his arousal.

Robin wanted to resist him. Knew she should resist him. That she should push him away, should once again ask him to leave.

But as he moved that hard arousal sensuously against her she felt the return of that moist heat between her thighs, groaning low in her throat as his tongue parted her lips even farther and plunged hard and hot into her mouth in a rhythm that matched his thighs as they moved so seductively against hers.

Her body felt consumed by liquid fire, every part of her alive and responsive to Cesare's slightest touch. Her nipples were hard and throbbing as he tore his mouth from hers, to lower his head and capture one of those hard peaks though her thin blouse and bra into the burning heat of his mouth, teeth gently biting even as his tongue moved moistly against that sensitive tip. Robin's spine arched as she sought a release for the spasms of pleasure between her thighs.

So aroused, so lost in that pleasure was she, that she could only stare up at Cesare dazedly when he suddenly raised his head to look down at her triumphantly.

'No, Robin,' he mused. 'I do not think sharing my bed will be unacceptable to you at all!'

His words, the scorn in his tone, made Robin feel as if she'd had a cold shower sprayed over her, so quickly did the heat of her arousal die. She pushed hard against him, almost stumbling as his arms immediately fell from around her and he stepped back to survey her with contemptuous eyes, his triumph at her capitulation more than obvious.

'You bastard!' she breathed furiously, her face

burning both at her response to him and at his obvious disdain at her response.

'Probably,' he accepted unconcernedly. 'But you will marry me, Robin. And soon, if we do not want the first of our children to be exactly what you have just called me,' he amended.

Robin felt embarrassed by her response to him seconds ago, angry with Cesare for being able to arouse her so easily, and not a little uncomfortable in her slightly damp blouse. She certainly wasn't in any sort of mood to put up with this man's supreme arrogance much longer!

'I have no intention of marrying you,' she gritted. 'Now or in the future!'

'Oh, but I think you will, Robin,' he contradicted softly. 'I think you will marry me very soon. And I think you will do so without any more histrionics.'

Robin looked at him searchingly—at his assured expression, the challenge in his gaze. His self-confidence was such that she sensed she hadn't yet got all the facts. 'What is it you haven't yet told me?' she finally voiced slowly.

'Intelligent as well as beautiful,' Cesare complimented her with a mocking inclination of his head—though he was not as unmoved by what had happened a few minutes ago as he liked to appear.

Robin Ingram really did have the most responsive body—a body that he knew had been on the point of orgasm when he'd decided to release her.

But he did not intend to make love to her in the sitting room of her father's home. He wanted to be in bed, both of them naked, when he gave Robin that release—wanted to lie and watch her, feel her, touch her as her body spasmed and trembled with pleasure. And then he wanted to lie back again, and watch her, feel her, as she gave him the same pleasure.

'What have I not yet told you?' he repeated consideringly, his teeth bared in a wolfish grin. 'How very astute of you, Robin, to realise I have saved the best until last.'

'Oh, cut the sarcasm and just get on with it!' she bit back impatiently.

His grin turned to a genuine smile. 'Sexual

frustration has not improved your temper, I see,' he observed in amusement.

Her eyes narrowed to purple slits. 'You have exactly thirty seconds to tell me why it is you're so confident that I'll marry you, after which I will call for the butler and have you removed—forcibly, if necessary—from my father's house!' she warned him heatedly.

'Somehow I do not think so,' he taunted confidently. 'But, nevertheless, I have no objection to satisfying your curiosity.' He gave a terse inclination of his head. 'In fact, it was always my intention to tell you exactly why it is you have no choice but to agree to marrying me.'

'I'm all ears!' Robin came back wearily, wanting this man gone. Not just from the house, but from her life!

She wanted to sit and lick her wounds—her battle scars!—in private, away from this man's all-seeing, all-knowing gaze.

'On the contrary,' Cesare Gambrelli continued derisively. 'Your ears, though charming, are far from your best feature.' His gaze moved slowly down to her breasts, lingering there.

It took all of Robin's will-power not to look down at her breasts too—to check and see if the material had dried enough yet after the caressing of this man's mouth for her nipples not to be clearly visible.

'You have ten seconds left!' she warned through gritted teeth.

He gave a confident smile even as he reached into the top pocket of his jacket, bringing out several pieces of paper that he began to unfold with infuriating slowness.

Robin watched him much as a fly must watch the spider that had caught it in its web. She was sure, from Cesare Gabrelli's unshakeable manner, that whatever those papers contained he personally had no doubts it was enough to induce her to accept his marriage proposal.

The marriage proposal that hadn't been a marriage proposal at all, but a statement of intent!

CHAPTER THREE

'Is it not time for you to call the butler, Robin?' Cesare Gambrelli prompted. 'I believe my allotted ten seconds are up!'

Yes, they were up, and they had passed slowly, painstakingly, as this man meticulously unfolded the sheets of paper he had withdrawn from his jacket pocket.

But her curiosity was such—as Cesare Gambrelli had known it would be!—that Robin had no intention of calling for anyone until she knew exactly what those papers contained.

'And I believe I told you to get on with it?' she came back tightly, so tense that her shoulders actually ached.

His mouth tightened. 'I do not care to have you, or indeed anyone else, tell me what to do!'

'Ditto,' she assured him tartly.

Cesare looked at her through narrowed lids, noting the pallor beneath her angrily inflamed cheeks, the way she held her body so rigidly, the telltale tremble in her tightly clenched hands.

All signs that she was not as calm or composed as she wished him to believe.

Perhaps he had pushed her enough for the moment. After all, he had plenty of time—years—in which to take his retribution.

'Very well,' he allowed. 'These papers—' he held them up for her to see '—gathered by me over the last three months, contain an accounting of all the IOUs and debts accrued in casinos scattered across Europe by your brother. Accounts that I have taken upon myself to satisfy—'

'I'm sure my father will be only too happy to see that you are reimbursed—'

'But I do not wish to be reimbursed, Robin,' Cesare assured her. 'At least not with money,' he added smoothly.

Robin's eyes widened. 'Those debts are the reason you think I will agree to marry you?' she said incredulously.

'To marry me and to become Marco's mother.'

Robin's resolve shook a little as he once again mentioned his now motherless nephew. It really was beyond imagining—a tragedy—that something so awful should have happened to a child of only a few months old.

And, despite her earlier protestations, she really wasn't as confident as she'd sounded when she had claimed the accident hadn't been Simon's fault…

The last three months had been traumatic. Her father had suffered a mild heart attack when told of Simon's death, and Robin's own grief at her loss had almost brought her to her knees.

But those three months had also been a time of learning just exactly how far Simon had fallen into debt. Robin knew that the whole situation had become a nightmare for the lawyers, who were still trying to sort out his will as each day seemed to bring in yet another claim for money owed to one establishment or another.

Obviously Cesare Gambrelli had missed those

particular claimants because most of them were in the UK.

But her father would find the money owed. And neither that, nor the spectre of Simon's debts in the first place, altered the fact that forcing her to become Marco's mother was not the answer to the problems that now faced Cesare Gambrelli as the adoptive father of his nephew!

There were no real answers for any of them with regard to the future. Three months ago two young people had died needlessly, prematurely, and though their families mourned them there was nothing they could ever do or say that would bring them back, or change what had happened.

It certainly wouldn't be solved by Robin agreeing to marry Cesare Gambrelli, she reaffirmed to herself determinedly.

Cesare watched the play of emotions on Robin's beautiful face—her uncertainty, her sorrow, quickly followed by a return of her earlier resolve.

It was time to end this cat-and-mouse game!

Cesare straightened. 'The debts and IOUs are

trivial, unimportant, in comparison with this,' he told her curtly, and he held out the top sheet of paper to her.

Her hands shook a little as she took the paper from him, all the blood draining from her face as she read what was written there.

'As you can see,' Cesare continued remorselessly, 'almost the last act of your disreputable brother Simon was to gamble away the shares that were left to him by your mother. Shares in your father's publishing company. Thirty per cent of the shares. Shares that are now owned by me, in a nominee account,' he pronounced, and he handed her a second sheet of paper.

Robin couldn't believe what she was reading. This couldn't possibly be true. Simon couldn't have—would never have—

Wouldn't he?

His gambling had become a sickness, an addiction. An addiction that Robin knew he had lost everything to. Everything, they had thought, except Simon's shares in their father's publishing company, left to him by their mother on her death five years ago…

'This can't possibly be legal—'

'It is perfectly legal, I assure you,' Cesare Gambrelli came back confidently.

She swallowed hard, glancing at those papers once again. 'But the money Simon received for them is—'

'Far beneath their value,' the arrogant Sicilian acknowledged dryly. 'Nevertheless, the transaction was completely legal, and would still have been so if your brother had accepted no more than one of your English pence for them!'

Robin felt slightly numbed, having no doubt that this man would never have come here so full of himself if he weren't absolutely sure his ownership was legal.

'I would be willing to gift these shares to you on our wedding day,' Cesare Gambrelli said with satisfaction.

Robin raised startled lids, staring at him incredulously. This man thought he could blackmail her into marrying him with the promise of the return of Simon's shares in her father's company…

He really did!

That darkly handsome face was set in grimly determined lines, his black eyes challenging as he stared at her levelly.

She shook her head. 'I'm sure my father will happily buy the shares back from you—at the full market value, of course,' she added hollowly.

'They are not for sale—for any price,' Cesare Gambrelli returned. 'At the moment, because as I told you the stock is held in a nominee account, my name is not registered as a shareholder with your family's company. However, if you do not agree to my terms, Robin, I intend to put them into my name and take up my role on the board. A very active role,' he finished pointedly.

Robin swallowed hard, not doubting him for a moment. Knowing how this man felt about her family, she was also sure that once he had taken his place at Ingram Publishing he would then do everything in his power to ruin the business—and her father!

The company meant everything to her father. He and Robin's mother had established it together, at the beginning of their marriage, building it up into the multi-million-pound empire that it was today.

It was a completely family-owned, family-run enterprise, Robin having worked there herself in the six years since she'd left university, and taken over as her father's assistant these last two years, since Simon's excesses had made him incapable of fulfilling that role.

'Your father was ill after your brother's death, I believe...?' Cesare Gambrelli enquired mildly.

Robin winced, not in the least fooled by the pleasantness of his tone, knowing this was yet another threat.

A very real one...

Her father had been instructed by his doctors to take things easy after his minor heart attack—advice he had been forced to ignore as each new day seemed to bring forth yet another disaster created by Simon's gambling excesses. In fact, her father was at yet another meeting this afternoon to discuss settling some of those debts...

She hesitated. 'I don't care to discuss my father's health with you—'

'I agree. There is no discussion necessary,' Cesare came back swiftly. 'I am sure that you know as well as I that the shock of learning to what extent his son gambled his life away would no doubt result in another seizure for your father—perhaps a fatal one—'

'What sort of man are you?' Robin cut in, aghast, her violet eyes accusing now in the paleness of her face.

'I am a Sicilian!' Cesare told her proudly. 'And in my country a blood feud such as ours can only be settled in one way! Blood for blood, Robin,' he explained flatly as she stared at him blankly. 'Paid for either in death or by a marriage between the two families!'

Her father had warned her to stay away from this man—although quite how she was supposed to have avoided him when he had actually come to their home, she had no idea!

But for now all she could wonder was how her father had known Cesare Gambrelli was such a threat to them. Whether he hadn't received some sort of response to his letter of condolence after all...

Cesare looked at her, completely unmoved by the pain and shock he could see in her face. His beautiful sister was dead, and this woman's brother, also dead, was the one responsible; he would have his blood payment, one way or another!

Robin paused, her throat moving convulsively before she answered him. 'My father would never agree to my marrying you under these circumstances—'

'The choice is not your father's but yours,' Cesare snapped dismissively. 'Refuse to become my wife and I will do everything in my power to destroy Ingram Publishing.'

It was not an idle threat on his part. As the next major shareholder of Ingram Publishing—after Charles Ingram's own fifty per cent—Robin was in possession of twenty per cent, her own inheritance from her mother... Cesare knew exactly what he would be capable of, concerning the disruption of the company. In fact, until he had met and decided he wanted Robin Ingram, and had realised there was another, even more satisfying kind of retribution than the one he had originally planned, he had been looking forward to bringing the Ingram company to its knees.

Now his primary desire was to bring Robin Ingram to her knees. Pleasurably so!

'But I don't want to marry you!' Robin cried protestingly.

He shrugged broad, unconcerned shoulders. 'Then I will take my place as a major shareholder of Ingram Publishing—'

'Why are you doing this?' Robin demanded emotionally. 'I can't believe that you want to marry me any more than I want to marry you! So why are you doing this?' she repeated desperately.

There were tears in her deep purple eyes now—tears that Cesare instantly distanced himself from; there was only one area of this woman's emotions that he wished to explore!

'My own wishes do not come into this—Marco is in need of a mother,' he reminded her detachedly.

'But as far as you're concerned I'm your bitterest enemy!' Robin reasoned quickly.

'You are making this too personal, Robin,' he cautioned.

'How much more personal could it get?' she came back, outraged.

'Oh, much more, Robin,' he assured her quietly, knowing she had understood him perfectly. 'But at this moment in time you merely happen to bear the name of my bitterest enemy— Ingram. And as a Sicilian—'

'A cold, vengeful Sicilian!' she put in insultingly.

He gave an acknowledging inclination of his head. 'Vengeful, perhaps. But I am not always cold, am I, Robin?' he queried tauntingly. 'And, despite what I have been told about the unattainable Robin Ingram, neither are you!'

She felt hot at his taunt, knowing she had be-trayed herself shamefully a short time ago, that her response to this man's kissing made it impos-sible for her to claim that, physically, she would be able to deny him everything.

She didn't like the fact, either, that there had obviously been gossip about her avoidance of all relationships since her marriage ended—gossip this man had clearly listened to. Even if he didn't know the reason she had chosen to remain aloof from all physical and emotional entanglement following her divorce...

'My father would never accept my marrying you for the reasons you've stated,' she repeated doggedly.

Cesare Gambrelli shrugged. 'I am not inter-ested in what your father would or would not accept!'

No, he wasn't, was he? Robin acknowledged heavily. It was of absolutely no concern to him whatsoever what she or her father felt about any-thing!

'But I am,' she told him determinedly. 'I know

my father well enough to know he would never accept my marrying a man I don't love as a means of saving his company from promised ruin.'

Yes, she did know him well enough to be sure of that. Just as she was equally sure that it would finish her father completely if, on top of Simon's recent death, and the debts and worry that had accrued since, his beloved company were to fail.

And she also knew him well enough to realise he would never accept her making the sacrifice of marrying Cesare Gambrelli in order to avoid that ruin!

Dear God, she wasn't actually thinking of *agreeing* to this man's archaic terms, was she?

No, of course she wasn't!

But until she'd had time to check into all of Cesare's claims she had no choice but to at least listen to him…

'Then it will be up to you to convince him otherwise,' Cesare Gambrelli—the man who was insisting on becoming her husband—said with a wave of his hand. 'I perfectly understand the reason you feel so…protective, towards your father—'

'Even if you don't give a damn yourself?' she accused angrily.

His eyes glittered darkly. 'I am not completely heartless, Robin—no matter what you may think to the contrary! I have no objection to your… *embellishing* the truth in order to satisfy your father's concern, if that is your wish. You may choose to tell your father we have fallen madly, passionately in love with each other. That you cannot live without me as your husband. Tell him what you like, Robin. But make no mistake, you will become my wife!'

He was so hard, so implacable—so damned sure he was going to get his own way, Robin recognised with dismay.

And wasn't he?

Could she really tell her father what Simon had done, of Cesare Gambrelli's demands, and risk her father having the second and perhaps fatal heart attack that his doctors had warned her might occur if he became too stressed?

Too *stressed!*

She had watched these last three months as her father had sunk deeper and deeper into despair with each damning action of Simon's coming to light following his death.

What she needed was time…

'I will give you some time to…become accustomed to the idea of becoming my wife,' Cesare Gambrelli told her graciously, even as he neatly folded those damning papers and put them away in his jacket pocket.

Time to think of a way out of this, Robin desperately finished her previous thought.

'I suggest the two of us have dinner together this evening in order to conclude the arrangements,' he said.

'You consider a mere few hours giving me time to become accustomed to the idea of marrying you?' Robin exclaimed.

Cesare looked at her, at the way she held her body so proudly—and he wanted nothing more than to finish what they had started earlier.

But he controlled his emotions. 'I do not see

the point in delaying the inevitable,' he stated practically.

'Inevitable to you, but not to me!' Robin fought back.

Cesare gave a thin smile. 'Marco is in need of a mother now, not in three, or even six months' time.'

And he, Cesare knew, wanted this woman in his bed. If she would not agree to it legally, then he would take her without the benefit of a marriage licence. *Then* he would marry her!

'I am obviously aware that you have been married before.' He spoke with distaste of her previous marriage. The thought of another man possessing all her passionate beauty was not in the least palatable to him.

'And what about you?' she attacked scornfully. 'You're what? Thirty-seven? Thirty-eight?'

'Thirty-seven to your twenty-seven,' he supplied tersely.

She nodded impatiently. 'And have *you* been married before too?' she challenged.

Cesare calmly surveyed her flushed beauty for

several lengthy seconds before answering her. 'If I had been married at all, Robin, then I would still be married,' he replied. 'Divorce is not something I will ever allow to happen in my life. Once married, I will stay married,' he added, snuffing out any hope that, once bound to him, with those shares safely in her possession, she could then decide to part legally from him.

The sooner he got her with child, binding her to him irrevocably, the better it would be for both of them.

'*You* will stay married,' he added, in case she had even the smallest doubt that he meant what he said. 'So, dinner this evening,' he repeated briskly. 'I think it would be best if I were to call for you here at seven-thirty—'

'I haven't even agreed to have dinner with you yet!' Robin cried frustratedly. Things were moving too fast for her altogether—Cesare Gambrelli was moving too fast for her altogether!

At the same time as she could feel the tightening of his ties about her as he drew her to his side with the intention of keeping her there...

True, at this moment in time she could see no way out of what he was proposing—ordering—her to do. But that didn't mean there wasn't one. And the more she played for time, the more chance she had of thinking of one!

He lifted dark brows, his mouth curved fully into a mocking smile. 'But you will, will you not?'

His confidence was just too—too infuriating! She felt like a mouse being played with by a very large, very dangerous feline! A black panther, perhaps...

Oh, get a grip, Robin, she instantly instructed herself. Cesare Gambrelli was definitely as dangerous as her father had warned her he was, but she had no intention of actually showing him how disturbed she was by his threats.

'Yes, I will,' she agreed through gritted teeth. 'But you will not come here and pick me up,' she told him, knowing she had to take some control of this situation or become completely lost to Cesare Gambrelli's demands. 'I'll meet you at the restaurant.'

Cesare's smile faded instantly, his mouth twisting derisively at what he easily guessed was a deliberate show of independence.

For the moment he had no problem with that— could allow her that freedom. He would have plenty of time, once she was his wife, to show her that he did not take orders from anyone— least of all the woman he was only taking as his wife in order to settle a blood feud!

'We will not be eating at a restaurant, but in my suite at the London Gambrelli Hotel,' he informed her loftily. 'I feel it would be…more private for the conversation we intend having,' he opined, before she had a chance to argue.

He could almost see the workings of her mind at this statement. First indignation. Followed by trepidation at the thought of being alone with him in his hotel suite. And then finally the realisation that, despite her reluctance, he was probably right.

Probably! He had no doubt whatsoever that this evening's conversation would be no less heated than the one they had just had. Just as he had no doubt that neither of them was the type of person to relish causing a scene in a public restaurant.

Her brother Simon had caused enough public scenes for the whole of his family.

Cesare's mouth tightened just thinking of the other man. 'I will expect you at the Gambrelli Hotel at seven-thirty.' Again he made it a statement rather than a request.

He could expect all he liked—Robin would get to his hotel this evening when it suited *her,* not him!

Pure bravado on her part, she accepted, even as she made the decision to deliberately keep him waiting this evening. Cesare Gambrelli had made it more than obvious that there was no way she was going to be able to avoid seeing him again, so what was the point in antagonising him?

It would make her feel better—that was the point!

If she could feel better about anything concerning this emotionally charged situation.

But, whatever time her father returned this evening, she intended speaking to him before she went out. Not with the intention of telling him about Cesare Gambrelli's visit, or his threats, but out of a need to know exactly what her father had meant by his warning that Cesare Gambrelli was dangerous.

Not that she doubted the claim for a moment. She now knew for herself exactly how dangerous he could be!

'Eight o'clock would probably suit me better,' she told him bravely.

He shook his head. 'That is far too late, I am afraid.'

Robin very much doubted this man was afraid of anything! 'Too late for what?' she prompted warily.

'Marco, of course,' he drawled. 'He is usually in bed by eight o'clock.'

Robin stared at him uncomprehendingly. 'You have Marco here with you in London?' she finally voiced weakly.

'But of course,' Cesare answered her. 'Where else would he be but with me?' He quirked dark brows challengingly.

Where else? Robin mentally echoed faintly. The prospect of having dinner with this man hadn't been all that alluring in the first place. But this was worse, so much worse, than she had even imagined.

She took a deep breath. 'I don't think it's a good idea for me to meet Marco just yet—'

'I am *sure* that you do not think it a good idea for you to meet Marco at all,' Cesare returned speedily. 'I am well aware that you have no experience with children, Robin,' he added. 'But it is a lack of knowledge you will have to overcome. And quickly.'

Robin was startled by this pronouncement. No experience with children…? Obviously, as the youngest sibling in her own family, she hadn't had an awful lot of experience with young children, let alone babies, but she would have loved one of her own.

'Well, it's true that I haven't been around young children much…' she began.

Cesare eyed her knowingly. 'Your marriage to the Honourable Giles Bennett was childless.

Which was surprising since, being the heir to his father's title, he needed children to continue his line. Maybe he divorced you because you refused him on that score? Perhaps, like many young women, you hoped to put off pregnancy and hang on to your freedom as long as you could?' He looked down at her with dark, searing eyes when he saw the way her expression visibly fell. 'But it is time you settled down now. You will soon overcome your selfish needs when you become my wife and Marco's mother,' he finished.

It was completely against Cesare's culture, and his own nature, not to cherish and adore children, and he had no sympathy with anyone who did not put them first.

Having set out to find out about Robin Ingram and Giles Bennett's divorce—and succeeding—Cesare knew his resolve to make her his wife, the mother of his children, had only deepened.

Although he hadn't quite expected such strong resistance from Robin to meeting Marco…

Not all women were maternal, he accepted that, and some took longer than others to settle down to motherhood. But somehow he didn't think that was really the case with the deeply responsive Robin Ingram.

She had obviously loved her older brother very much, and her affection for her father was unmistakeable, so perhaps it was that she feared pregnancy and childbirth?

Whatever her reasons for not wanting to get on and have babies, she would get over them.

Because Cesare expected—fully intended—her to mother his nephew and to produce a brother or a sister for Marco within the first year of their marriage....

CHAPTER FOUR

'YOU ARE LOOKING very beautiful this evening,' Cesare complimented Robin formally, as he ushered her out of the private lift that opened straight into his hotel suite at seven forty-five.

Robin eyed him distantly, having deliberately adopted her role of cool and unattainable by wearing a simple black dress that covered her from her throat to just above her knees. Her hair was smoothed back from her creamy brow and fastened in a neat chignon, exposing the plain gold earrings she wore, and a simple linked bracelet was her only other jewellery. Her make-up was deliberately light—only mascara, a sheer foundation and peach lip gloss.

After all, she had thought as she'd surveyed her reflection in the mirror before leaving home, she wasn't going out on a date. This evening was probably going to be just another challenging conversation with Cesare Gambrelli.

And it would introduce her to Marco…

She drew in a deep breath. 'I hope you aren't expecting me to return the compliment?' She dismissed his own darkly attractive appearance in a black silk shirt and black trousers as she swept past him and into the sitting room of the suite.

A penthouse suite, she had discovered after making enquiries at the reception desk downstairs, that consisted of the whole of the top floor of the building, with a private lift to whisk her to its lofty heights.

But what else had she expected? Cesare Gambrelli was one of the richest men in the world, and he could easily afford to keep the top floors of all of his exclusive hotels around the world for his own private residences if he so chose. Which he probably did.

Cesare's gaze followed Robin admiringly as he followed her into the sitting room. Whatever her lack of composure earlier today, Robin Ingram had definitely regrouped, looking every inch the beautiful, haughty socialite that she was as she moved to stand in front of one of the giant windows that looked out over the sunset-dappled capital.

'Drink?' He held up the bottle of champagne he had ready and chilling in a silver ice bucket.

It was later than seven-thirty, of course. But he had expected that. He'd known that Robin would deliberately be later than the time he had specified, if not as late as she had said she would be, in an attempt to show him that she would not fall in with his plans.

Not yet, anyway…

'Champagne, Cesare?' she came back teasingly. 'Isn't your…celebration a little premature?'

'Is it?' he mused unconcernedly, and he poured some of the pink bubbling liquid into a glass for Robin before filling his own and carrying them both over to where she stood. 'I make a point of always drinking champagne, Robin,' he explained as he handed her one of the flutes.

She returned his gaze unflinchingly. 'How wonderful to be so privileged!'

Cesare smiled lazily down at her. 'Not at all. I have found it is the only alcohol that does not result in a hangover!'

He was so damned sure of himself, wasn't he? Robin fumed, as she sipped the pink bubbly wine. So confident that he had the upper hand in their dealings with each other.

And didn't he?

It hadn't been easy introducing the subject of Cesare Gambrelli with her father when Charles had returned home earlier this evening. In fact, it had proved almost impossible. Charles had merely repeated his warning for her to stay away from him when she had mentioned Cesare's name. A comment he wouldn't enlarge on, despite her urgings.

Although it really wasn't too difficult, after the conversation she'd had with Cesare herself that afternoon, to realise why her father was wary of their family's tenuous connection to this man. The one concession her father had made to his near-silence on the subject of Cesare Gambrelli was to state that the other man was completely ruthless in his business dealings.

But just how much more ruthless would he be towards the family he held responsible for his sister's death?

But, without alerting her father to the fact that Cesare Gambrelli had paid her a personal visit that very afternoon, she hadn't been able to press him for any more information.

Neither had she told him that Cesare was the 'friend' she'd said she was meeting for dinner this evening; that would have certainly sparked off a conversation she wasn't yet ready for. Besides, her father had looked so tired after yet another meeting to discuss Simon's gambling debts...

'What shall we drink to, Robin?' Cesare drawled derisively. 'A successful conclusion to our earlier conversation, perhaps?' he added, with a mocking smile at her obvious resentment at being there at all.

Her eyes glittered deeply purple as she looked up at him from between thick, dark lashes. 'That would only result in *your* making the toast!'

Cesare gave an appreciative grin. 'I have a feeling that we will be doing a lot of things in conflict for some time to come, Robin. But we may as well begin now, do you not think? Drink up,' he added impatiently as her fingers merely tightened about the slender stem of the glass.

Instead of doing as he requested she chose to walk away from him, moving across the room to stand beside the door.

As if poised for flight, Cesare easily guessed. Well, what was the saying? She could run but she couldn't hide. Robin could try running from him all she wanted, but his mind was completely made up: this woman would become his wife.

His eyes moved slowly down her body. He knew she had probably chosen to wear that black sheath of a dress as a means of detracting from the graceful lines of her body. As she had also chosen to smooth back and confine the wild beauty of her honey-gold hair.

Unfortunately for Robin it had the opposite effect; there was something extremely tantalising in the wearing of a dress that hinted at her curves rather than displayed them, and the taming of her hair merely made him want to release those glorious honey-gold tresses and kiss her until she became totally pliant in his arms.

She would probably be most displeased to learn that her efforts at killing any desire he might feel for her body had only succeeded in increasing his need; he had to know, to caress and kiss every velvety-soft inch of her!

Robin wished Cesare would stop looking at her in that way. She was feeling completely physically vulnerable under the intensity of his dark, narrowed scrutiny—as if he had stripped every article of clothing from her body. And there wasn't much; she was only wearing black panties and silk stockings beneath the dress.

She shifted uncomfortably, aware that her body was responding to his caressing assessment in spite of herself. Her nipples were hard and sensitised beneath the soft material of her dress, and there was a spreading warmth between her thighs.

It was totally incomprehensible to her why she

reacted to this man in the way she did. Goodness knew, she had earned that 'unattainable' label these last twelve months, and yet every time she was near Cesare Gambrelli her body responded as if it already knew his—as if they were already lovers!

'I have ordered dinner to be served at eight-thirty,' he told her lightly, continuing to sip his own champagne even as he continued to look at her with that dark, penetrating gaze.

He could order dinner for whenever he liked—Robin wasn't in the least sure she would be able to eat anything. Just being with this man was totally robbing her of her appetite.

'Fine,' she dismissed tautly, although what they were supposed to do for the next forty-five minutes was questionable!

Surely Cesare didn't expect them to spend all the time before dinner with his baby nephew?

'You seem a little…tense this evening, Robin,' he observed.

Tense? She was so taut with anxiety about this whole evening that her body ached, and her fingers gripped so tightly about the champagne glass that she was in danger of snapping its thin stem!

'After the way you threatened me earlier, how do you expect me to feel, Cesare?' she retorted.

His mouth thinned. Of course he had threatened this woman earlier—she was the sister of the man whose memory he held in the highest contempt, the man responsible for Carla's death!

He arched dark brows. 'Perhaps you would like me to give you another demonstration of how much you will…enjoy being married to me?' he invited smoothly, instantly rewarded by the look of alarm in her violet-coloured eyes.

'I haven't agreed to marry you yet,' she reminded him waspishly. 'So any sort of *demonstration* on your part is totally unnecessary!'

Cesare was lingeringly aware of the rapidly beating pulse at the base of her throat, of the soft rise and fall of her pert breasts, of the way her dress hinted at the enticing warmth of her shapely thighs.

'It may be unnecessary, Robin,' he acknowledged as he took a step towards her, 'but I, for one, find it inevitable.'

He took the champagne flute from her unresisting fingers to place it on the coffee table with his own, before turning back to draw her into his arms as his head lowered and his mouth easily captured hers.

The curves of her body fitted so perfectly against his. Her breasts crushed against the hardness of his chest, the softness of her thighs pressed hard against his arousal, and her hair fell in silky waves about her face as he reached up and released it from its confinement.

Her mouth tasted of champagne and honey. Her lips were soft and responsive. So very responsive!

This had to stop, Robin told herself achingly.

Had to!

But for the moment she had no will to bring an end to Cesare's assault on her mouth. His tongue was moving in a sensuous caress against her bottom lip as he quested for entry—an intimacy she couldn't deny him as her lips parted and his tongue plunged into the waiting heat of her mouth.

Dear God, she wanted this man! she acknowledged, as her fingers became fiercely entangled in the dark thickness of his hair.

She wanted Cesare as she had never wanted any man before—not even Giles, the man she had been married to for three years. The man who had cast her aside when she no longer suited his plans for the future—

She wrenched her mouth from Cesare's. 'No!' she protested, even as she pushed against him. 'I don't want this.' She breathed raggedly, glaring up at him as his arms remained like steel bands about the slenderness of her waist, moulding her body to the hardness of his.

'No?' he taunted knowingly, eyes dark, a nerve pulsing in the rigidness of his jaw.

'No,' she repeated firmly.

Cesare noted the slight trembling of her bottom lip, knowing that she lied—that at that moment she wanted him very much.

As he wanted her.

But she was right. This was not the time. Perhaps later, once Marco was asleep…

He released her abruptly to step back. 'It is time that you met Marco,' he told her haughtily.

'Now?' she breathed shakily, her fingers arresting in the movement of smoothing back her hair as she stared up at him with a haunted expression.

Cesare's mouth tightened at her obvious reluctance. 'Yes—now,' he grated. 'I will go through to the nursery and get him—'

'Oh…couldn't I just come through with you and say goodnight to him there?' she suggested. 'It seems a pity to disturb him if he's already tucked in,' she added lamely.

'He is not in his cot yet,' he assured her firmly. 'And even if he were, I am sure, like all children, he would welcome this break in his routine.'

No escape there, then, Robin acknowledged with a grimace, her emotions too battered by Cesare's kisses for her to even attempt to hide the fact that meeting his baby nephew was an ordeal she would rather have forgone.

'I will only be a moment,' Cesare assured her distantly, before turning to stride from the room.

Robin picked up her glass of champagne before moving back to stand in front of the window, seeing nothing of the magnificent view outside as she took several nerve-bolstering sips of the wine.

What would he be like, this young nephew of Cesare's? If he looked anything like his uncle then she had no doubt that he would be a handsome baby—

He looked *exactly* like his uncle! Robin acknowledged achingly, having turned sharply to look at Cesare as she heard him come back into the sitting room, the little boy held securely in his arms.

Marco's hair was as dark as Cesare's, with the same silky curl, and his eyes were that same dark chocolate brown. His beautiful face creased into an excited smile as he looked across the room and spied her standing in front of the window, revealing two endearing little white teeth in his bottom gum.

He looked very tall for six months, his long legs and body encased in a cartoon-patterned babygro, his little hands resting trustingly on his uncle's chest.

Robin felt her insides melt just looking at him…

'Let's go and say hello to Robin, Marco,' Cesare murmured encouragingly, and he walked across the room towards her with the baby still held firmly.

Robin took an involuntary step backwards, her back instantly coming into contact with the window behind her, its slight chill sending a shiver down her spine.

Cesare's mouth tightened as he saw Robin back away from him as they approached, the way in which she quivered with distaste even as her eyes remained riveted on Marco.

What was wrong with this woman? Apart from caring for Carla when she was a baby, Cesare had had little contact with babies himself, but he had fallen in love with Marco from the moment he was born. He could not believe it possible for anyone not to do the same once they had seen the tiny boy.

But Robin no longer looked as if she just wanted to run, but as if the devil himself were chasing at her heels!

Cesare's mouth hardened. 'He does not bite, Robin,' he said pointedly.

'No?' she came back tautly. 'Those teeth say otherwise.' She attempted a lightness she was obviously far from feeling.

Cesare looked at her searchingly, noting the way she held herself away from them, as if she were afraid even to touch Marco.

But Marco obviously had other ideas, gurgling happily as he reached out his small arms towards Robin.

'Cats do the same thing, I believe,' Cesare observed, as Robin seemed to shrink even further into herself.

'What...?' she breathed shakily, with barely a glance at him as she continued to stare at Marco as if hypnotised.

Cesare shrugged his shoulders as he maintained his hold on the now squirming Marco. 'They have an unerring instinct to go to people who show a dislike for them!' he explained sharply, and his young nephew launched himself at Robin in the total belief that she would catch him.

Something she did most reluctantly, holding the baby slightly away from her as Marco made a grab for the long honey-coloured hair that Cesare had so recently released from its confinement.

Cesare's gaze was deliberately unreadable as he looked down at the two of them.

Carla had been a natural mother, totally at ease with her baby son from the moment he was born. But Robin looked as if she was holding a time bomb in her arms—one that was set to explode at any moment.

Marco knew no such inhibitions, grinning at Robin unconcernedly as he twisted a long length of her hair into his baby fist and talked to her in the gibberish that only he could understand.

Cesare frowned darkly and held himself ready to take his nephew from her if it became necessary. If—as she looked in danger of doing!—Robin collapsed completely.

Unless this was just a ploy on her part to try and shake Cesare's resolve to marry her in order to settle the blood feud between their two families?

He had made no secret of the deep love he had for Marco, and Robin was intelligent enough to know that he would have no desire to present the baby with a mother who didn't even want to hold him, let alone laugh and play with him.

Was Robin using his love for Marco against him?

If she was, then she was in for a disappointment!

'I will take Marco back to bed now,' Cesare told her coldly.

Robin turned to give him a startled look, having briefly forgotten Cesare was even in the room, all of her attention focused on the baby she held in her arms.

'He seems quite happy where he is,' she pointed

out ruefully, and Marco turned to grin at his uncle as his fingers tightened in her hair.

'Nevertheless, it is past his bedtime,' Cesare informed her reprovingly. He reached out to take the resisting baby from her, Marco's happy gurgles instantly turning to cries of protest.

Robin reached up to untangle the tiny fingers from her hair. No easy feat when Marco seemed determined not to let go.

'Perhaps I had better come to the nursery with you…?' she offered huskily as Marco continued to grip.

'Perhaps you had,' Cesare allowed wryly, resisting his nephew's efforts to return to Robin's arms as he strode off towards the nursery. Robin had no choice but to hurry after him if she didn't want her hair pulled out by the roots.

Marco grinned at her over his uncle's shoulder, still hanging on to her hair, and Robin returned that grin now that she was no longer under Cesare's close scrutiny.

Because Cesare had been wrong earlier today

when he had claimed her marriage to Giles had ended because she'd avoided getting pregnant.

She hadn't avoided it at all.

She hadn't been able—*wasn't* able—to give Giles the children he wanted to carry on the Bennett name.

Robin hadn't been too worried when she didn't conceive during the first year of her marriage—had just assumed that it would happen when it happened. But as the months passed with no sign of a baby, Robin had decided she ought to visit a medical specialist.

The first of many such visits.

There had followed two years of tests. The keeping of charts. Followed by more tests.

But no baby.

The tests had shown that there was nothing wrong with either Robin or Giles's fertility—that Robin simply hadn't conceived. Her specialist had advised that perhaps they should think of adoption, that sometimes in cases like theirs, where no reason could be found for the lack of conception, with the pressure taken off the mother became pregnant quite naturally. Giles had refused to even consider adoption, had wanted a child of his own blood or not at all.

That child—a son—had been born to Giles and his second wife only two months ago…

Leaving Robin with the certainty that *she* had to have been the one at fault.

The end of her marriage meant that she would never have a child now, that she was doomed to a marriageless and a childless future. For how could she marry any man and expect him to accept that she could never give him a baby?

Except that Cesare Gambrelli, although he didn't know it, was now offering to marry her and give her the child she couldn't have herself.

A baby she had fallen in love with on sight!

CHAPTER FIVE

'COULD I POSSIBLY…freshen up before dinner?'

Cesare turned at Robin's halting request, which intruded on his dark and brooding thoughts as the two of them left Marco's nursery together a few minutes later.

He had thought he would catch her off guard by presenting Marco in that way, and yet Cesare knew that *he* was the one who felt unsettled by the encounter…

It really was totally inexplicable to him why Marco had taken such a liking to Robin; she had certainly done nothing to encourage him.

The baby had screamed when Cesare had returned him to his cot, his little arms reaching up imploringly to Robin. But Robin had remained completely detached as Cesare laid the baby down, before tucking him beneath the covers with his favourite teddy bear at his side.

Robin's aloofness towards Cesare he could understand and excuse, but her coldness towards Marco he could not accept. The baby had already lost his mother—even if he wasn't really old enough to have realised it—and Cesare had no intention of allowing Robin to maintain that ridiculously cool attitude towards him just because she wasn't in control here.

Because, no matter how she might wish it otherwise, he still had every intention of making Robin his wife. And sooner rather than later!

'Use the bathroom there.' He gestured dismissively and he continued to stride towards the sitting room, definitely feeling in need of more champagne.

'Thank you,' Robin accepted quietly, before escaping into the bathroom.

When she looked at her reflection in the mirror over the sink, she could see her eyes were overbright.

She was in love!

Not with Cesare Gambrelli.

Nor with any other man.

But with a six-month-old baby who had captured her heart at first sight!

She sat down weakly on the side of the bath, breathing deeply in an effort to calm her racing pulse.

Marco was adorable—absolutely adorable. And it had felt so good when she'd held him in her arms, so achingly right; he was the baby she had dreamt of having for so long—so much so that she had been reluctant to relinquish him to Cesare when the time had come.

What did she do now…?

Cesare Gambrelli had told her he intended marrying her. That he intended for her to be Marco's mother.

How she wanted the latter, if not the former…

But the price was being Cesare's scorned and despised wife—a woman he had only married to settle what he called a blood feud. Did she want that?

Yes!

Cesare didn't know it, but he was offering her something she had thought she would never know—a joy Robin had thought for ever denied her. Now that she had met Marco, held him, felt the warmth of him, been the recipient of his beautiful smile, there was no way she would be able to walk away from the chance to be his mother.

She knew she daren't let Cesare see how deeply her emotions had been affected, already knowing him well enough to realise that if he thought he was actually giving her something she so desperately wanted, then he would use that advantage to bend her totally to his arrogant will.

Yes, now that she had seen and held Marco she fully intended marrying Cesare— but it would be on her own terms, not his....

'We may as well go through to dinner,' Cesare announced when Robin rejoined him in the sitting room, her hair once more in a neat chignon and looking again like the coolly detached woman who had arrived at his apartment less than half an hour ago.

Once Robin was his wife, Cesare had decided as he sipped his champagne and waited for her to rejoin him, he had no intention of giving her any choice but to become Marco's mother. With time, he hoped she would learn to be at ease with with the child, to love him as he deserved to be loved.

'Fine,' she accepted distantly, before preceding him into the dining room that he indicated.

A woman any man would be proud to have on his arm, Cesare knew, as he watched the gentle sway of her hips as she walked in front of him.

Or in his bed…

'Have you decided what it is you wish to tell your father about our forthcoming marriage?' Cesare prompted, once he had seen her seated opposite him at the small, intimate table he had requested be laid for their meal together.

Robin eyed him warily. 'I believe I told you earlier that nothing has been settled yet concerning a marriage between the two of us?'

Cesare gave a hard smile. 'Fight it all you want, Robin, but the marriage *will* take place.'

She hadn't given herself away, Robin realised

with relief. And she dared not do so, either, because if Cesare even half guessed at how she had fallen for Marco, then all her bargaining power was spent. And she had little enough to start with!

'Perhaps,' she allowed uninterestedly, avoiding the intensity of his stare as she placed her napkin across her lap in preparation for eating the platter of seafood that was the first course. 'As for how we deal with my father...' she paused, as if to give the matter some thought '...I really don't think he would accept anything less for me than what he perceives as a love match.'

Cesare's eyes widened. 'I know I told you earlier that I would go along with whatever you decided to tell him, but do you seriously expect me to behave in front of your father as if I have fallen in love with you?'

'Beyond your powers, is it?' Robin came back tauntingly, stung by his tone of incredulity. 'Or just totally incomprehensible to you?' she added softly as she saw his contemptuous expression.

'You can't pretend to be in love because you've

never *been* in love—is that it?' she prompted curiously.

'Love!' he snorted. 'My father loved my mother so much that when she died he drank himself to an early death! Carla loved Marco's father—and he abandoned her totally once he knew she was expecting his child! Contrarily, your own husband did not want you once you had refused to have his child. I do not need to have been in love, Robin, to know it is a destructive emotion!'

Robin had been prepared to give him an argument on the subject—until he mentioned her own marriage. Because she *had* loved Giles when she'd married him—had thought he loved her too. But that love hadn't been strong enough to withstand Giles's disappointment when she hadn't been able to give him the child he wanted...

And she already knew that falling in love with Cesare Gambrelli would be sheer madness—for *any* woman!

No, loving Marco, and being this man's unwilling wife, was as far as she was willing to go.

'True,' she acknowledged. 'Nevertheless, for

my father's sake, I really think if we are to go ahead with this marriage that we will have to behave for a few weeks as if we're in love with each other.'

Cesare looked at her frustratedly, knowing what she was demanding was her own price for agreeing to marry him without further argument or delay. A high price, granted, and not one that he would normally have even considered. But perhaps the pretence would have benefits to himself that even Robin had not considered yet...

He gave an arrogant inclination of his head. 'In that case I suggest we begin the pretence this evening, with your not returning to your father's home as expected. It will tell him, without any word having to be spoken between the two of you, that you have taken a lover.'

Robin sat back in her chair to look at him admiringly. 'Touché, Cesare,' she finally admitted ruefully. 'No one could ever accuse you of losing control of a situation, could they?' she added wryly.

Losing control in any situation was never in Cesare's plans.

He had taken many women to his bed, and considered himself a considerate as well as attentive lover for as long as his interest lasted. But all his relationships had been completely under his control. His emotions, other than desire, had never been engaged.

And, no matter what he might decide to pretend for the sake of her father, they would not be with Robin, either.

Love made fools of people—as it had his father and Carla. It was a trap that Cesare never intended falling into.

He shrugged. 'I suggest that once we have eaten you call your father and inform him you will not be returning tonight.'

At which time, as Cesare meant him to do, Robin knew her father would draw his own conclusion.

Charles would probably be pleased with the development too.

He had made no secret of his concern about

the way she had become almost reclusive since her separation and divorce, burying herself in her work at Ingram Publishing and avoiding a social life, and would probably view any sign of her being involved with a man as a good thing, rather than something he should be concerned about.

Until he learnt that Cesare Gambrelli was the man she was involved with, of course—when his reaction would probably be completely the opposite!

But she would deal with that later. For now she had to concentrate on getting through this evening, on talking to her father on the phone before staying the night in one of the many bedrooms in this penthouse suite of the Gambrelli Hotel—

Unless…

She looked across at Cesare with accusingly suspicious eyes. 'I have no intention of sharing your bedroom tonight, Cesare!' she told him determinedly.

He raised his dark brows calmly. 'I did not ask you to.'

'I'm quickly learning that you don't ask—you just take!'

Cesare eyed her mockingly, enjoying this angrily rebellious Robin much more than the icy socialite who had arrived at his suite a short time ago. 'I can assure you I do not intend for you to share my bedroom tonight,' he drawled.

She didn't look at all convinced by his reassurance. As she should not. His assurance that she wouldn't share his bedroom did not mean that he didn't intend to share *hers*...

'Come, Robin,' he encouraged briskly as he picked up the fork beside his plate. 'Let us eat our food and talk of more general things. Was the charity dinner a success last weekend?'

She still felt suspicious as she picked up her own fork. 'Very much so,' she finally confirmed. 'In fact, one anonymous benefactor—who coincidentally couldn't stay for the dinner—left us a donation of fifty thousand pounds,' she explained, with a pointed look in his direction.

Cesare smiled. 'It was for a good cause.'

She nodded. 'Disabled children.'

Cesare's mouth tightened. 'You think me as uncharitable as your father does?' he rasped.

Robin wasn't really sure what she thought of this man any more. He was obviously the anonymous donor, and his love for Marco was unquestionable, and yet for reasons of retribution he was also capable of forcing a woman he didn't love, who didn't love him, to marry him.

He was an enigma.

One that held an inexplicable fascination for her.

She had certainly found herself thinking about him more than she should the last few days!

'Only to people called Ingram,' she came back challengingly.

'Then it is as well that your name will soon become Gambrelli, is it not?'

She looked across at him for several seconds before sighing. 'As you said, Cesare, let's eat,' she replied, and she avoided meeting his eyes.

He remained very still and silent for several long, tense seconds, Robin only breathing comfortably again when he finally joined her in eating.

'You do not like oysters?' he asked several minutes later, as Robin pushed her plate away without even attempting to touch the two succulent shellfish that remained on the platter.

Robin gave him a knowing look. 'If you think they'll do you any good, you're quite welcome to them!' she came back tartly, well aware of the aphrodisiacal reputation oysters possessed.

'Oh, I think two will be quite enough for one night,' he returned sardonically.

Well, that attempt at mockery had backfired on her, hadn't it? Robin acknowledged to herself, as Cesare stood up to remove their plates, standing close beside her as he did so, his warm proximity making her shiver slightly.

Perhaps staying here tonight wasn't such a good idea…

After all, just because she was going to tell her father she was staying out tonight it didn't mean it actually had to be here, in Cesare Gambrelli's hotel suite, did it?

Of course it didn't.

'Would you like me to do that?' she offered as she looked across to where Cesare was taking the serving dishes containing their main course from the trolley, feeling more confident now she had made the decision to leave.

'Why not?' He straightened as she stood up to join him beside the trolley. 'The sooner you become accustomed to your wifely duties the better, hmm?' he added provokingly.

There was one 'wifely duty' she knew she would never become accustomed to!

There was no way she would ever be comfortable as this man's lover…

Oh, physically she wanted Cesare; there was no way she could deny that after the way she responded to his slightest touch. But she had always believed that physical pleasure should be accompanied by love. She had been a virgin on her wedding night, and had taken no other lovers since her marriage ended, either.

'Perhaps,' she began slowly, as she served thinly sliced beef fillets and vegetables onto their plates, a large portion for Cesare, a much smaller one for herself, 'it's time we discussed the terms of this as yet mythical marriage…?' She placed the plates on the table in front of them before sitting down again.

'I have already agreed to satisfy your father's… sensibilities concerning a marriage between the two of us,' Cesare replied. 'I do not think you are in any position to dictate any further terms to me, Robin.' Though he admired her nerve, he had absolutely no sympathy for her sentiment.

'Nevertheless,' she told him firmly, 'if I do agree to marry you—and it's still a big if—then I also intend having some input into the…nature of the marriage.'

Cesare found himself smiling, sure that he knew exactly which part of the marriage she was referring to. 'Go on,' he invited dryly, deciding he had better quickly eat some of the delicious beef in front of him. From the little experience he had of dealing with this woman, his appetite could desert him at any moment.

Her chin rose defiantly, those violet-coloured

eyes glittering purple. 'Perhaps we could start by having you drop this mocking way you have of responding to everything I say!' she snapped.

His smile widened. 'Perhaps if you stopped coming out with comments that I find amusing, I might be able to do so,' he came back laconically.

'I'm glad you find it so amusing, Cesare!' Robin glared. 'Personally, I find absolutely nothing to laugh about in this situation!'

Yes, he had been correct—he was losing his appetite.

For food, anyway…

He liked that heated flush to her cheeks, the way her eyes sparkled deeply purple with emotion, her breasts thrusting against the thin material of her dress as she tensed her shoulders with indignant reproval at what she viewed as his inability to take her seriously.

But he seriously wanted to strip that dress from her body right now and make love to her!

'I am not laughing, Robin,' he assured her

huskily. 'But perhaps we should postpone this conversation until after we have eaten?'

'I'm not hungry!' She pushed her plate away, her whole body rigid with her anger.

Neither was he. His appetite was for something much more…tactile than food now.

'Do not behave like a child, Robin,' he said sternly.

'Is that what I'm doing?' she came back swiftly.

'I believe so,' he responded.

'And if the great Cesare Gambrelli believes it to be so, then it must be so!' Robin scorned.

Cesare looked at her consideringly. 'Why are you deliberately provoking an argument between the two of us, Robin?' he finally asked.

'I'm being provocative, am I?' she said heatedly.

'You must know that you are.'

Because Robin *knew* she wanted him!

Because she had seen the way he had looked at her seconds ago, seen the desire in his eyes before he'd masked it, and at this moment her whole body was singing with the knowledge of her own need!

Because she didn't want to want him!

'Forgive me.' She didn't even attempt to hide her sarcasm. 'Obviously I become a little argumentative when a man is blackmailing me into his bed!'

Cesare's breath hissed from between his clenched teeth. 'Your primary roles as my wife will be as Marco's mother and as my lover!'

'I don't wish to become your lover at all!' Robin told him with conviction, even as her body warmed in betrayal of her claim.

'All evidence is to the contrary, my dear Robin.' Cesare raised an eyebrow.

'Bastard!' she breathed furiously, stung by his confidence. 'Bastard, bastard, bastard!' she repeated recklessly, and she stood up to glare down at him. 'I dislike you intensely, Cesare Gambrelli—'

'Perhaps you should once again show me how much you dislike me, Robin?' he invited, as he too stood up to move purposefully around the table towards her.

Too far. She had gone too far, Robin acknowledged as she began to back away from him.

She had meant to get him to listen to her, to have him take her requests seriously, not provoke him into this totally physical response.

Hadn't she?

As her pulse leapt, the breath caught in her throat, and Cesare's mouth captured hers in a kiss that was hot, hungry and sensually demanding, allowing her no opportunity to deny her own response.

His tongue slid intimately into her mouth, stirring her body into throbbing awareness, and Robin wasn't sure what she had intended any more—only knew that she didn't want this to stop, that she needed this man's lovemaking in a way she had never needed or wanted any other man.

Her lips widened and she kissed him back hungrily, her hands becoming entwined in the dark thickness of his hair as she held him to her, her tongue duelling with his as she pressed her body into him.

Fire. This woman was pure, molten fire. And Cesare wanted to lose himself in her flames. As he wanted her to lose herself in the inferno that raged inside him.

He deepened his kiss and freed Robin's hair once again to entangle his hand in its silky scentedness. His other hand moved the length of her body restlessly as he touched and caressed her slender curves. Feeling her quiver of response, he raised the hem of her dress and began to caress a path upwards.

She breathed low in her throat as his hand touched the bare flesh above her stockings, that sigh becoming a groan as that hand moved assuredly towards the warmth between her thighs.

Cesare's fingers easily pushed aside the silk of her panties, and he touched the silky curls before moving unerringly to the centre of her desire, touching her, feeling the way she instantly blossomed and opened to him.

Wet. Robin was so wet. So wet and ready.

Cesare continued to kiss her as he untangled his other hand from her hair, moving that hand to the back of her dress, lowering the zip down the length of her spine to allow the dress to fall in a heap at her sandalled feet. He bared the pert arousal of her breasts to his caress, finding she fitted perfectly into the palm of his hand. His thumb moved to caress the fiery peak, and he could feel the moistness increase between her thighs as his fingers stroked the throbbing nub of her arousal.

Robin had been lost from the first touch of Cesare's mouth on hers—had no will to fight the volcanic passion that had been burning barely beneath the surface between them all evening. Her breathing was shallow as Cesare moved his mouth from hers and bent to capture her hardened nipple between his lips, teeth and tongue, tasting before he suckled her deeply into the heat of his mouth, at the same time as his finger moved into the heat between her thighs.

Her breath became a sob as she moved rhythmically against him, the earthquake building deep within her, increasing her thrusts against him as her shuddering release convulsed around and against his stroking hand—a release that seemed to go on and on as Cesare continued those caresses, filling her whole body with a bone-melting pleasure that she never wanted to stop....

CHAPTER SIX

WAS THERE ANY dignified way in which she could extract herself from this situation, Robin wondered with aching embarrassment seconds later, as her composure slowly returned to her.

No, there wasn't, she decided, feeling a cringing awkwardness at her total lack of control. For one thing, she was wearing only panties, stockings and her evening sandals, while Cesare was still dressed in his black silk shirt and trousers.

Not that he looked completely together, she realised, as she looked at him from beneath lowered lashes: his shirt was unbuttoned where her questing fingers had sought to touch his bare flesh, and his dark, overlong hair was slightly tousled from the way those same fingers had become entangled in its thickness as she'd clung to him. There was a flush of arousal on his high cheekbones.

An arousal that he hadn't satisfied.

That *she* hadn't satisfied!

It might have been some time since she'd known a man intimately, but she knew she had never been a selfish lover, that a lack of physical consideration for her partner was not something Giles had ever been able to accuse her of.

Although she could never remember responding to her husband in the abandoned way she had to Cesare!

But, although only minutes had passed, wasn't it just a little too late for her to even attempt to give Cesare the release that his throbbing body, pressed against hers, so obviously craved?

'What are you thinking now?' Cesare's voice was harsh in the pregnant silence that had grown between them.

Robin hesitated before answering. 'That this is the most embarrassing moment of my entire life,' she told him honestly.

'Embarassing?' Cesare repeated, standing back

slightly to look at her, her hair rumpled and silky, her eyes overbright, her mouth slightly swollen from the force of his kisses. Her breasts were still aroused from the touch of his hands and lips, and there was a lethargy to her limbs that spoke of recent arousal and release. 'You are beautiful, Robin,' he assured her. 'In fact, once we are husband and wife, I wish for you to hate me in that way every night of our married life!'

'You're so sure, after…after that…that I'll marry you, aren't you?' she accused with an indignant glare, and she bent down to snatch up her dress from the carpeted floor and hold it against her bare breasts.

Cesare sensed that she was once again being deliberately provocative, but the unsatisfied ache of his own body meant he was in no mood for yet another argument.

There was no way Robin could deny her physical response to him, or his response to her, and any more prevarication between them was pointless.

He gave a sharp inclination of his head. 'I suggest you tell your father we are to be married as soon as a special licence can be arranged—'

'Oh, you *suggest,* do you?' Robin echoed sarcastically as she pulled her dress back on and zipped it firmly back into place.

'Yes—I—suggest,' Cesare repeated forcefully, the familiar ache of his body certainly not improving his temper.

What should have happened now was for the two of them to go to bed together and finish what they had started. But one look at Robin's rebellious expression told him that definitely was not going to happen!

No matter. He had the rest of their lives together to take his fill of this highly sensuous woman. A few days, perhaps weeks, to wait; delay would only make his anticipation all the sweeter...

'At least give me some credit for having the sense not to make it an order, Robin,' he grated.

She gave a derisive snort. 'I have no intention of giving you credit for anything, Cesare!'

He quirked dark brows over mocking brown

eyes. 'Not even for being a considerate lover?' he taunted softly.

'For being an experienced one, you mean!' she came back self-disgustedly, and her cheeks burned anew at his reminder of her earlier loss of control.

And something else, if Cesare was not mistaken. Perhaps she had not had the same consideration for his own pleasure?

'I have had other lovers, yes,' he conceded. 'But then, so have you…'

'One lover,' she corrected. 'I would never— That…what happened just now would never have happened if—' She broke off suddenly. 'I have to go,' she muttered almost inaudibly.

It wasn't what they had planned for tonight, Cesare knew, but in view of what had just ocurred he was inclined to let Robin make her escape.

Before, no doubt, spending a frustratingly restless night himself.

Although there was some sweet consolation for him in the fact that Robin claimed her only lover had been her ex-husband…

It was a surprise, a very pleasant surprise, and her uninhibited response to him encouraged him in the belief that Robin would accept him as a husband much sooner than she thought she would.

'Very well, Robin,' he conceded. 'I will allow you to—'

'You aren't *allowing* me to do anything, Cesare,' Robin cut in impatiently. 'My God, you're arrogant,' she added disgustedly. 'I'm leaving now because I want to, not because you're allowing me to! Don't think—don't *ever* think—that you'll control me with physical pleasure, Cesare. Because you won't!'

Had that been his intention? However, the physical pleasure they had just known together was not a weapon to be used but to be enjoyed—reveled in, even.

Did Robin think—did she really not know—that the pleasure she had experienced tonight was much rarer than people would have you believe? That, no matter what all those glossy magazines might say, many women went through the whole of their life without experiencing a single orgasm in the arms of their lover. Pleasure, yes, but not necessarily the deep, orgasmic response that Robin had just given so freely.

He was not about to refuse the gift she had given him, let alone throw it back in her beautiful face!

'Just go, Robin,' he told her sternly. 'With your agreement,' he added, 'we will meet again tomorrow evening—'

'At a restaurant this time!' she came back swiftly, eyes flashing angrily.

He gave a humourless smile. 'At a restaurant this time,' he conceded. 'Do not ever think you will control *me* with physical pleasure either, Robin,' he warned.

Her eyes widened briefly, followed by a frown, before she turned on her heel and marched out of the room.

Cesare heard the lift doors open and then close seconds later as she left.

No matter.

He had tomorrow night. And the night after that. And all the other nights for the rest of his life....

'You spent yesterday evening having dinner with *who?*' her father said incredulously, as he sat across the breakfast table from Robin the following morning.

'Oh, Daddy,' she replied, her tone teasing, 'As I know there is absolutely nothing wrong with your hearing, I'm sure you heard me the first time.' She raised mock-reproving brows, her elbows resting on the table as she cradled her morning cup of coffee in her hands.

Although she hadn't exactly had dinner with Cesare—or at least they had never finished eating!—she inwardly acknowledged ruefully, still writhing with embarrassment inside herself every time she so much as thought of the time she had spent in Cesare's arms the previous evening.

Nothing like that had ever happened to her before.

Oh, the physical side of her marriage to Giles had been satisfying enough at the beginning. Less so as they'd become caught up in the tests and charts and temperature-taking that had been part of their effort to conceive the child Giles so wanted. The child Robin had wanted too…

That she was now going to have in Marco, if her marriage to Cesare Gambrelli took place.

And now she'd met Marco, she had every intention that it would.

She had woken up this morning—in her own bed, thank goodness—filled with what she could only describe as a feeling of satisfied langour. Caused by Cesare's lovemaking, she knew.

But it was that langour, the knowledge that when she and Cesare were married she would become his wife in the full sense of the word, as well as her joy in the prospect of becoming Marco's mother, which had encouraged her to start the awkward process this morning of breaking the news of their relationship to her father.

The sooner he knew, the sooner she could become mother to that enchanting little boy.

Her father looked stricken by her news as he stared across the breakfast table at her. 'I— But… Cesare Gambrelli, Robin?' he finally burst out disbelievingly. 'I wasn't aware that you even knew the man!'

'You introduced the two of us last Saturday at the charity dinner, remember?' she reminded gently.

'Well, yes, but—' He shook his head. 'When did the two of you meet up again?' His brow furrowed.

Robin was aware that this conversation was going to be delicate, to say the least, and also aware that Cesare wasn't the most patient of men—that if she didn't talk to her father then Cesare surely would. It would be so much better coming from her.

'He called at the house to see me.' She deliberately didn't say he had come only yesterday. 'To invite me out to dinner. And I accepted.'

'He came here?' Her father's face was very pale.

'Yes.' Robin tilted her head to one side. 'Is there

some reason why he shouldn't have?' She kept her tone deliberately light.

Her father stood up to pace the room, still in his dressing gown as it was Saturday morning and he didn't have to go in to work—although he had brushed his hair and shaved before coming down to breakfast.

'Perhaps I should have talked to you about this earlier, Robin,' he admitted, 'but I had no idea you and Gambrelli would ever meet again after the charity dinner. Damn it, I *hoped* you would never meet again! You see, Robin, the other driver involved in Simon's accident—'

'Was Cesare's young sister, Carla,' she interrupted calmly. 'Yes, I know.'

'You know?' her father breathed, and he stopped his pacing.

She nodded. 'Cesare and I have talked about it—'

'You've talked about it?' he repeated.

'Daddy, I'm sure we'll get much further with this conversation if you stop repeating everything I say. And, yes,' she sighed, 'Cesare and

I have talked about the accident—about Simon and Carla's deaths. Strangely, it only encourages both of us in the belief that the two of us were meant to meet...'

She was laying it on a bit thick, Robin knew, but for his own sake she really did have to convince her father that her relationship with Cesare was a love match, and not the vendetta against the Ingram family that it really was.

Her father looked desperately upset just at the thought of her going out with Cesare Gambrelli. How much more upset would he be if he knew his beloved only daughter was being forced into a marriage with this man?

Or at least it *had* been coercion on Cesare's part...

Meeting Marco, holding him in her arms, being captivated by the warm innocence of his baby smile, had changed all that.

She refused to allow that the pleasure she had found last night in Cesare's arms might also have had something to do with her change in attitude...

'Daddy, wouldn't it be wonderful if something good could come out of that tragedy?' She looked up at him appealingly, slightly ashamed of herself for using such feminine wiles on her father—he never had been able to resist the appeal in her violet-coloured eyes—but ultimately knowing it was for the best.

Better that her father should voice his reservations about her relationship with Cesare now, and have those reservations allayed, than he should learn the real reason she was seeing the other man and then absolutely refuse to let her comply with Cesare's demands.

'Well, yes, of course it would...' Charles acknowledged distractedly. 'But I wrote to the man after the accident, you know. The letter came back inside another envelope a week later—ripped into four pieces!' He grimaced. 'I had the distinct feeling he would rather have plunged a knife into my throat!' he added with a shudder.

So, Cesare *had* received her father's letter of condolence, and had obviously read it—before returning it in a way that could only be perceived as a threat.

No wonder her father had warned her to stay away from Cesare!

She gave a rueful smile. 'Cesare can be a little...dramatic, can't he?' She forced the sound of affection into her voice. 'It's all that Latin blood,' she continued brightly. 'But I can assure you that he's no longer angry about what happened.'

Her father looked sceptical. 'Are you absolutely sure about that?'

'Positive.' She beamed reassuringly, putting her cup down to stand up and give him a hug. 'Now, take that frown off your face and be happy for me. I'm hoping to introduce Cesare to you as your future son-in-law some day soon!' she told him gaily.

'You're going to *marry* the man?' her father said disbelievingly.

'If he asks me.' Robin nodded. 'And I think he will.'

'But you said you were never going to marry again! That no man would want you because you can't give him children—though I've never be-lieved that,' he told her firmly.

'But that's the wonderful thing about Cesare,' Robin came back brightly. 'He already has a male heir to inherit, so it isn't going to matter that I can't give him children of his own,' she dis-missed, not inclined to get into a discussion of exactly who Cesare's heir was.

In fact, it might be better if she changed the subject altogether! 'Keep your fingers crossed for me, hmm, Daddy?' she encouraged happily.

Her father still looked as if he would prefer to lock her in her bedroom and keep her there until Cesare Gambrelli had disappeared from London altogether. But, as he really wasn't about to do that, he had no choice but to accept what she told him.

'Just take care, Robin?' he said gruffly, and he laid his hand on her cheek affectionately. 'I'm not sure I altogether trust Gambrelli's motives.'

'Don't be silly.' She smiled confidently. 'And of course I'll be careful,' she assured him, feeling her heart aching at the deception she was practicing on her father, but knowing it would ache even more if he were to discover the truth and forbid her to marry Cesare, and so force Cesare into carrying out his threat against Ingram Publishing.

No, it was much better this way, she reassured herself.

She had no intention of showing Cesare any of that compliance when she met him at Gregori's restaurant later that evening, as they had arranged during a very brief telephone call earlier in the day. Had no intention of making this any easier for Cesare than she already had with her response to him the previous evening.

'Did you sleep well last night?' Cesare prompted tersely, once the ordering of champagne and food was of the way.

'Very, thank you,' she came back briskly. 'You?'

Little wildcat, Cesare fumed inwardly. He knew damn well she only had to look at him to see the dark shadows beneath his eyes and the lines of strain beside his nose and mouth and know that he hadn't slept. At all. Instead he had prowled his hotel suite until the early hours of this morning, going down to the gym when it opened at six o'clock to work off some of his excess energy, if not his sexual frustration, on the rowing machine for an hour.

Robin, on the other hand, looked fresh and alert this evening; the deep purple dress she wore was the same colour as her eyes, her hair hung loose about her shoulders, and she had huge gold hoops in her earlobes, her deep peach lip gloss silkily inviting on those sensually pouting lips.

An invitation that made Cesare want to wipe everything from the table between them, lay Robin upon its surface, and bury himself deep inside her!

'Do not play with me, Robin,' he warned icily. 'I am not in the mood for games.'

'Dear me—sexual frustration hasn't improved your demeanour, has it?' she saucily pointed out, before turning to give the wine waiter a glowing smile as he poured some champagne into a glass for Cesare to taste.

Cesare took a sip of the wine before placing the glass back on the table. 'It is corked,' he said coldly. 'Bring me a sixty-three. Chilled to the correct temperature this time.'

'Yes, sir. Of course, sir.' The startled wine waiter grabbed the bottle and two glasses and hastily back away.

'That wasn't kind,' Robin reproved softly once they were alone.

His eyes glittered darkly as he scowled across the table at her. 'I thought we were both agreed that I am not a kind man.'

Robin didn't remember them ever agreeing on that, but Cesare certainly hadn't been very polite to the wine waiter. The poor man was probably a gibbering wreck in his wine cellar at this moment, as he desperately checked the temperature of the second bottle of champagne before serving it!

'I will leave him a large tip at the end of the meal, if that will make you feel better, Robin,' Cesare compromised.

'Well, no, it isn't really a question of making

me feel better, now, is it?' she reasoned lightly, very aware of the fine edge to Cesare's control. 'I'm not the one you were rude to.'

'I was not rude—' He broke off as the man once again appeared beside their table, sighing deeply at his flustered removal of the champagne cork. 'It is not your fault that the previous bottle of wine was…unacceptable,' he assured the waiter smoothly, very aware that there had been nothing wrong with the first bottle of champagne at all, that he had only verbally bit out at the other man because Robin had smiled at him so warmly.

Her smiles, and everything else about her, belonged to him!

Not that she had given many smiles in *his* direction, but Cesare found he deeply resented her bestowing her good humour on anyone else, either.

He had never been possessive where his lovers were concerned. His previous relationships had always been brief, never lasting longer than a month or two, and at the first sign of any serious intent on the woman's behalf he would end the affair and move on.

This slight possessiveness he felt where Robin was concerned had to be because she was to be his wife, and as such he would require exclusivity, he assured himself.

'There, now.' Robin smiled at him mischievously once the wine waiter had left their table, the bottle of wine completely satisfactory this time. 'That didn't hurt too much, did it?'

'I did not apologise because you thought that I should,' he told her haughtily. 'I merely realised I was not…polite to him earlier,' he accepted curtly.

No, he hadn't been, Robin acknowledged—but she doubted that too many other people had ever told this man when he was being impolite, let alone reproved him for it as she had…

She sat back as their first course was placed on the table—pâté for Cesare, smoked salmon for herself—very aware that several other women in the restaurant had looked at Cesare admiringly when they'd arrived together a short time ago, and that several of those women were still eye-ing him covetously.

He did look rather tall, dark, and handsome tonight, she allowed ruefully, with that overlong dark hair curling silkily onto the collar of the pale grey shirt he wore beneath a charcoal grey suit. His dark good looks and those dark brown eyes were riveting, to say the least, and the ex-pert tailoring of his suit showed his wide shoul-ders, tapered waist and thighs to their advantage.

Something that at least half a dozen other women in the restaurant seemed just as aware of!

'This marriage you're proposing between the two of us, Cesar—' she kept her gaze lowered on her smoked salmon '—is it to be an exclusive relationship? Or are you expecting me to ignore the odd mistress or ten?' She looked up at him challengingly as she said the last.

Cesare had been in the process of eating some of his toast and pâté, but he put it back down on his plate as he frowned across at her. 'Would it bother you if I was?' he probed softly.

She pulled a face. 'No one likes to be made

to look a fool. I just thought it might be better if I was aware of the…arrangement beforehand, that's all.'

No, it was not all, Cesare reflected darkly. If he were to take mistresses during their marriage, then no doubt Robin would consider she had the same freedom to take a lover, or lovers. But, as he had never shared a lover, neither did he intend sharing his wife.

'There will be no mistresses, Robin,' he vowed. 'I have no idea why you should think there would be when I will have a perfectly desirable wife waiting for me at home. Now, do you think we could eat our meal this evening without the danger of the indigestion I am sure both of us suffered yesterday?' he added, before she could come back at him with any of her clever replies.

Robin raised blonde mocking brows. 'I've already told you—I slept perfectly well last night.'

Cesare glared at her frustratedly for several long seconds before leaning forward across the table to easily hold her startled gaze with his. 'Perhaps I should warn you that at this moment this tabletop is looking very tempting as a place to make love to you!' he hissed between gritted teeth.

Those purple eyes remained locked with his for several long, expectant seconds, like a deer caught in the headlights of a car, and the sexual tension between them was so strong Cesare felt as if he could almost reach out and touch it.

'Good—I see that we understand each other.' He finally nodded his satisfaction at her silence, his teeth showing very white as he smiled. 'Now, could we eat our food? Please?' he requested dryly, as he remembered her reaction to anything she construed as an instruction on his part.

Robin's hand shook slightly as she picked up her fork and began to eat her smoked salmon, not even tasting its delicacy as she recognised the sexual awareness that was once again singing through her veins.

She had never been so aware of anyone in her life as she was Cesare, and she wondered what it meant.

If it meant anything!

She could just be one of those frustrated women who suffered from sexual starvation at the end of their marriage. Especially as she knew now exactly what a wonderfully satisfying lover Cesare was…

'I spoke to my father about you this morning,' she ventured, once they had eaten their first course and the plates had been taken away.

Cesare raised dark brows. 'In what way?' he prompted guardedly.

She grimaced. 'I told him that you had ravished me last night and now I *had* to marry you! In what way do you *think* I spoke to him about you, Cesare?' She sighed her impatience with his suspicion.

He shrugged wide shoulders. 'You could have decided to tell him of my…intentions towards Ingram Publishing.'

'Hardly likely, after all the trouble I've already gone to to keep it from him—'

'Trouble?' Cesare repeated in a dangerously quiet voice.

Robin's cheeks flushed uncomfortably, and she

knew he had to be referring to the time she had wantonly spent in his arms yesterday evening. 'I merely told my father that we have been seeing each other since the two of us were introduced last weekend,' she snapped. 'And that when—if—you propose to me, I intend accepting.'

Cesare gave a humourless smile. 'And how did Charles take to the possibility of having me as a son-in-law?'

'Badly.' Robin didn't even attempt to prevaricate. 'But he'll come round,' she added confidently.

'I admire your optimism,' Cesare drawled.

It was impossible not to admire this woman, Cesare acknowledged. She certainly hadn't backed off from his threats, and now she had opened the subject of their relationship with her father too. Which he appreciated could not have been easy.

'Perhaps if you hadn't sent his letter of condolence back quite so—aggressively?' she reminded him.

Cesare's mouth tightened. 'My sister had

been dead a matter of months; I was not feeling…kindly disposed towards anyone, let alone a member of the Ingram family.'

In fact he had felt murderous at the time. Carla had gone for ever, and Marco had been left completely parentless—although Cesare still hadn't given up on finding the man who had deserted Carla when she'd most needed his support; he had a private investigator looking into exactly who had been his sister's lover fifteen months ago. Because he would find Marco's father, and when he did—

'My father—both of us—we were suffering too,' Robin reminded him huskily.

Yes, he could see that now. Cesare realised that Robin and her father had still loved the reprobate that Simon Ingram had become, that they had felt his death as keenly as he had felt Carla's.

But that realisation changed nothing.

Made absolutely no difference to his own plans to make Robin his wife.

In fact, Cesare was even more determined on that resolve since last night!

CHAPTER SEVEN

'I'M STILL NOT absolutely convinced this is a good idea,' Robin told Cesare later that evening, as the two of them went up to his hotel suite in the private lift.

He eyed her mockingly as he leant back nonchalantly on the other side of the lift. 'Scared, Robin?' he taunted.

'Of you? No,' she asserted, even as her fingers tightly gripped her evening bag. He wasn't the one she was scared of—it was her own response to him that scared her. 'I'm just not sure my father is ready for me to stay out all night, now that he will naturally assume I'm with you.'

'You are twenty-seven years old—'

'But I'm living in my father's house at the moment,' she returned swiftly.

Cesare shrugged, standing back to let her vacate the lift first once it had stopped at the pent-house floor. 'You still have time to change your mind.'

Yes, she did, not having made the phone call to her father yet to tell him she wouldn't be back tonight.

But, despite her uncertainty about exactly where in this spacious hotel suite Cesare would expect her to sleep—or not, as the case might be—Robin knew that she didn't want to change her mind.

Her uncertainty about Cesare's intentions apart, she just might see Marco again, might have the chance to hold him again as she had been aching to do since meeting him yesterday.

'If it makes you feel better, Robin, I do not con-sider it…appropriate for us to share a bedroom tonight,' Cesare rasped, impatient at her ponder-ing silence. 'Marco's nursemaid is obviously also in residence, and as I intend for the two of us to be married… It is not appropriate,' he repeated hardly. 'And it is not flattering to me as a lover for you to look so relieved at the thought of not sharing my bed,' he finished disgustedly.

Had she looked relieved? Robin wondered. Maybe. But not for the reason Cesare obviously thought; it just somehow seemed completely unacceptable that she responded so wantonly to a man who was forcing her into marrying him by threatening her family.

'I was merely concerned that you might not benefit from missing another night's sleep,' she told him with a saccharine-sweet smile.

Cesare eyed her admiringly, not fooled for a moment by her insincerity. 'A lot can happen before bedtime, Robin,' he pointed out, rewarded by the delicate blush that instantly coloured her cheeks. 'I will pour us both a glass of brandy while you call your father,' he told her as he strode into the sitting room, deliberately giving Robin the privacy to make her call.

If he were Robin's father—which he was not, thank goodness!—then he would have his concerns about her apparent choice of lover too.

Robin was frowning when she walked through

to the sitting room several minutes later. 'I spoke to the butler,' she explained as she took her glass of brandy from Cesare. 'He said my father seemed rather weary this evening and had retired early,' she explained distractedly.

'You think there is reason for concern?' Cesare frowned.

Robin shook off her feelings of despondency to look up at him angrily. 'Don't pretend that you actually care, Cesare!' she challenged. 'Not when only yesterday you were quite prepared to ruin my father's publishing company and probably kill him in the process!' she reminded him accusingly.

Cesare's expression darkened, a frown between those almost black eyes, his mouth a thin, disapproving line. 'Must I remind you that I am not the one responsible for your father's current ill health?' he responded.

No, Robin acknowledged heavily; that had been caused by her father's worry over Simon's obsession with gambling, followed by his death.

Although possibly her own failed marriage and then her divorce hadn't helped the situation.

Whatever the reason, her father was still obviously under a lot of strain—which only seemed to confirm her decision to keep Cesare's plans for Ingram Publishing from him.

She took a reviving swallow of her brandy before answering, 'I've been trying to think of a way to return the shares of Ingram Publishing to my father—after we're married, of course—without his ever becoming aware that they had gone out of the family's possession—'

'Do not trouble yourself, Robin,' Cesare cut in arrogantly.

'But I *do* trouble myself, Cesare,' she retorted. 'It will defeat the whole object of my…of my decision to marry you, if my father were ever to realise Simon had gambled his shares away.'

'Of your sacrifice, I am sure you meant to say,' Cesare drawled derisively.

'Don't attempt to put words into my mouth, Cesare!' Robin threw back, her eyes flashing deeply purple. 'If I had meant to say sacrifice, then I would have done so, I can assure you!'

Yes, he was sure that she would, Cesare noted. Robin's frankness was one of the qualities he most admired about her...

'The significant part of your previous statement concerns the fact that your father might realise,' Cesare told her dryly. 'But there is absolutely no reason why he should,' he assured her. 'Simon sold the shares to maintain his gambling obsession, I bought the shares from the casino owner, who happens to be an acquaintance, through my broker—'

'How convenient!' Robin couldn't resist her sarcastic rejoinder.

Cesare's eyes darkened warningly. 'I bought them,' he repeated evenly. 'On our wedding day they will be gifted back to you. At which time you are perfectly at liberty to destroy all evidence of them ever having been out of family ownership,' he completed with finality.

'You really do have all of this worked out, don't you, Cesare?' Robin observed.

Not all of it, no—Cesare knew that he certainly had not been prepared for Robin Ingram, nor the desire he felt to make love to her every time he was with her.

As he did now!

'Perhaps it is time we went to our respective bedrooms,' he bit out tersely. 'I have several business meetings to attend in the morning, and I need to read some papers tonight before going to sleep.'

Robin was surprised at the abruptness with which Cesare was bringing an end to the evening. She had been prepared for—had expected—a repeat of last night's lovemaking before the two of them parted.

Was she just a little disappointed that Cesare felt no such inclination?

Of course she wasn't!

Was she?

Well…maybe a little, she conceded reluctantly, as she placed her empty brandy glass firmly down on the coffee table. Which was pretty stupid of her. This wasn't a love affair; she was being *forced* to accept Cesare's marriage proposal!

'Which bedroom would you like me to use?' she prompted tartly.

His mouth twisted wryly. 'I would suggest the one that adjoins my own, but I accept that might be misconstrued too!'

By whom? Herself? Or Marco's nursemaid?

Not that it mattered. The truth was that Robin was the one in danger of spending a sleepless night this time, as she imagined a naked Cesare in the bedroom along the hallway from her own— meaning she would probably be feeling as irritable tomorrow morning as he had this evening!

'A chaste kiss goodnight is permissible, however,' Cesare murmured mockingly as he watched the play of emotions on Robin's face.

The unattainable Robin Ingram most definitely wanted him physically!

He gave a satisfied smile, his own disappointment no longer as uncomfortable now that he knew Robin would be in the bedroom along the hallway from his own tonight, suffering the same sense of deflation.

'A chaste kiss goodnight!' she echoed. 'No, thanks. I think I'll pass,' she said. 'If you'll just tell me which bedroom I'm to use, I'm sure I can find my own way...'

'Do not be childish, Robin,' Cesare chided softly as he crossed the room to her side.

Her eyes sparkled angrily as she returned, 'I said I'll pass on the chaste kiss, thanks!'

'I was referring to the fact that you have pulled me up about the politeness of showing a guest to her bedroom, not your reaction to a chaste goodnight kiss,' Cesare told her, his rebuke rewarded by the flush of embarrassment that coloured Robin's cheeks.

'A guest, Cesare?' she repeated unbelievingly. 'I would hardly call myself that.'

'Nevertheless, for tonight that is exactly what you are,' he insisted tautly.

'Fine,' she accepted tersely.

It was not fine. It was far from fine. But it was all that Cesare could do for this evening.

Marco's nursemaid, Catriona, who came from their native Sicily, had been with Carla from the day of Marco's birth. As Cesare expected one day to take Robin and Marco back to Sicily, if only for a visit, he considered that his wife's reputation should be unsullied by any gossip which might take place between Catriona and her family. His sharing his bedroom with Robin before they were married, even for the night, was definitely not acceptable.

'The goodnight kiss does not have to be completely chaste...' Cesare offered throatily, standing very close to Robin once he had shown her to one of the four bedrooms in the suite—his room, Catriona's and Marco's nursery taking up the other three.

Robin's lids narrowed as she looked up at him, slightly unnerved by his proximity, able to feel the warmth of his body so close to hers, the smell of his aftershave tantalising her senses. 'Either a kiss is chaste or it isn't, Cesare,' she replied. 'I really don't think there can be degrees of chastity!'

His mouth twisted ruefully. 'Perhaps I was a little hasty earlier…?'

Robin felt her earlier bad temper evaporating as she saw the way Cesare's eyes had darkened to black, his lids slightly lowered as that gaze locked hungrily on her slightly parted lips.

He really had been serious about the necessity of not scandalising Marco's nursemaid by the two of them sleeping together tonight! And she had thought he was just paying her back for his own feelings of frustration the night before…

'No, you were perfectly correct, Cesare,' she told him. 'It really wouldn't be appropriate for us to sleep together.'

'Who said anything about sleeping?' he said huskily.

Robin laughed softly even as she gave him a light push in the chest that took him back out into the hallway, quickly closing the bedroom door behind him to lean back against it, almost able to feel his brooding presence on the other side of that door. Her own feelings of frustration were nowhere near as deep now that she knew Cesare wanted her too....

Robin awoke with a feeling of complete disorientation, taking a few seconds to realise where she was—in a bedroom in Cesare's suite—let alone the reason she had woken so suddenly.

It was still dark outside, and it was obviously still the middle of the night, so she couldn't understand what—

And then she heard it again—that faint, totally unfamiliar sound of a baby.

Marco!

Robin lay in the bed for several minutes longer, hearing the sound twice more and wondering if Catriona had woken and gone in to Marco, or if he was alone. It wouldn't hurt to at least check, now, would it?

She pulled on her panties and dress, not bothering with her stockings or her shoes, padding along the hallway in her bare feet to listen outside Marco's bedroom door.

He seemed to be talking softly to himself now,

rather than actually crying, which was something—although Robin still wasn't sure whether or not he was alone. She couldn't hear another voice, but perhaps Catriona was being quiet in an effort to get the little boy to go back to sleep.

Robin opened the nursery door quietly before peering inside and noticing that the room was lit by a single night-light plugged into the wall. Marco was alone, clearly visible in his cot, those dark brown eyes so like his uncle's, lighting up excitedly as he spotted Robin in the doorway, and at once launched into the garbled chatter that only he understood.

'Shh, baby, or you'll wake everyone else,' Robin crooned softly as she hastily entered the nursery and closed the door behind her, before moving to the side of Marco's cot. 'Can't you sleep, little man?' She smiled down at him, her heart turning a somersault in her chest as he beamed warmly back at her, falling down onto his bottom onto the cot's mattress as he held up his arms to be picked up.

Robin didn't quite know whether she should

pick him up or not. Marco seemed to be wide awake, and she doubted he would simply lie down and go back to sleep now that he knew he wasn't alone. But Cesare might not approve of her taking Marco out of his cot in the middle of the night...

When she married Cesare, Marco would be her son too, and if she wanted to pick him up in the middle of the night then she would, damn it!

And she did want to pick him up—so much wanted to hold his warm little body against her again, to hold and cuddle him as she would never be able to hold and cuddle a baby of her own.

Oh, he felt so good, she acknowledged achingly as she lifted him up to walk across to a chair and sit down with him still cradled in her arms. She nuzzled her face into his neck, his skin so soft and pliant, smelling of soap and talcum powder.

Marco giggled as her warm breath tickled his neck, his laugh one of pure enjoyment as his arms moved about her neck and he held on tight.

Robin's heart melted inside her, unbidden tears

springing into her eyes as she fell more in love with this adorable baby than ever.

And if—*when*—she married Cesare, Marco was going to be hers. Her own beloved baby. Her son!

Marco was touching her hair again now, seeming fascinated by its honey blondeness as he curled it about his fingers, quite at ease as he sat on her knee and talked in his own special language.

Robin had no idea how long she sat with him, playing and talking, making him giggle all over again as she blew gently on his obviously sensitive neck. Time didn't matter. She never wanted to let Marco go, and was choking with emotion as he eventually grew tired and laid his head down on her shoulder to fall asleep in her arms, his tiny fingers still holding on tightly to her hair.

The tears fell silently down Robin's cheeks as she sat in the chair just holding him. But they were tears of happiness for the maternal fulfilment she had thought would never be hers. For the gift of this beautiful little boy who already held her heart in the palm of his hand.

She wasn't aware of falling asleep too, but daylight shone in through the window when she woke for the second time. Marco was still asleep in her arms—arms that had continued to hold him close even as she slept.

She couldn't be found here, Robin knew—couldn't allow Cesare to see how she cared for Marco. Cesare already had the upper hand in their dealings by being in possession of the Ingram Publishing shares. How much more dictatorial would he become if he were to realise how she really felt about this adorable baby?

She stood up to carry Marco across to his cot, reluctantly laying him gently down before tucking the covers over him. She lingered in spite of herself, unable to stop looking at him as he lay so angelically beautiful, longing to smooth those dark curls, to touch his creamy cheek, but knowing she didn't dare be here when he woke again, that she didn't dare risk giving her feelings away to Cesare.

Too much rested on Cesare not knowing that she already loved Marco, Robin accepted heavily as she reluctantly turned to leave the nursery. Cesare believed her to be immature and selfish, that it had been her choice to put off having children. And until they were married, until she had those shares in Ingram Publishing firmly in her hand, she didn't dare let him see otherwise.

'What are you doing?'

Robin's breath caught in her throat as she turned to look at Cesare striding forcefully down the hallway to where she had just closed the nursery door softly behind her.

He looked thunderous, as if he suspected her reasons for being in Marco's nursery were less than innocent.

Her chin rose as she frostily met his dark, accusing gaze. 'I thought I heard Marco cry,' she defended herself.

Cesare looked down at her searchingly, noting the pallor of her face with no make-up, the defiant glitter in those violet-coloured eyes, the stubborn set of her mouth.

He had woken at his normal seven o'clock, knowing he would have time to shower, shave and dress before Marco woke at seven-thirty. He usually spent half an hour or so having breakfast with his nephew before he had to leave for any business meetings.

He certainly hadn't expected to leave his bedroom and see *Robin* emerging from Marco's nursery!

Considering the reason Robin's marriage had ended, and her ambivalence towards children, it was the last place Cesare would have expected to find her...

'And did you?' he prompted, and moved past her to open the nursery door and glance inside.

Marco was fast asleep in his cot.

Cesare's gaze was once again accusing as he turned back to Robin after softly reclosing the door. 'Obviously not,' he grated.

'Obviously not,' she echoed, in an almost defiant tone.

Cesare's eyes narrowed speculatively. He was not altogether sure he believed Robin's explanation, but was unable to think of any other. 'Do not fear, Robin. There will be time enough for you and Marco to become better acquainted once the two of us are married,' he assured her sardonically.

'I'm not frightened, Cesare,' she came back hardly. 'Of you or your nephew!'

Fear was the last thing Cesare wanted her to feel for him.

Although he was sure he had seen something like fear in her eyes just now, as she'd left Marco's nursery…

Could it be that Robin actually *feared* caring for a young baby?

'It is my intention that Catriona continues to care for Marco after the two of us are married,' he informed her huskily.

It was Robin's turn to look at him with puzzlement, to wonder why he was reassuring her of such a thing when he had earlier declared that caring for Marco, for Carla's motherless baby, was to be part of her punishment for their blood feud.

Didn't Cesare even trust her to be around Marco?

As if she would ever harm a glossy dark hair on that adorable baby's head.

She resented Cesare for even thinking such a thing!

'I'm sure that in your usual arrogant way you will continue making whatever decisions you want after the two of us are married,' she said. 'Well, you can make them, Cesare—but that doesn't mean I'll obey them! Now, if you will excuse me—' she turned away '—I think it's time I was leaving— What are you doing?' she demanded indignantly as he grasped her arm and turned her back to face him.

He maintained that grip on her arm, his jaw clenched, his eyes dark as he looked down at her. 'You are saying I am arrogant?' he rasped.

Robin gave a choked laugh. 'Saying? You *are* arrogant, Cesare. In fact, you're the most arrogant man it's ever been my misfortune to meet!' she added.

Those dark eyes glittered warningly. 'Misfortune, Robin?' he repeated softly.

'You don't seriously think that a little kissing on your part has made me any more eager to be your wife, do you, Cesare?' She shook her head even as she gave him a pitying look. 'If you do, then let me assure you that you have seriously overrated your powers of sexual persuasion!'

The damned *arrogance* of the man! The gall! Hadn't she already told Cesare that he would never rule her with the physical pleasure she'd experienced in his arms?

His mouth thinned as he continued to look down at her for several long, penetrating seconds, before his hand released her arm and he stepped away from her. 'I find I have become tired of this delay before our marriage, Robin,' he announced. 'I am appreciative of the fact that you are close to your father—'

'You should be, because it's the only reason I'm here!' she came back heatedly.

His face darkened. 'I would go carefully, if I were you, Robin—'

'Or what?' she challenged.

'You are once again being deliberately provocative,' he warned her. 'But this time it is a provocation I intend to ignore. I will come to your father's house this evening so that we can discuss the date of our wedding.'

'I'm twenty-seven years old and divorced. Don't you think asking my father for my hand in marriage might be a little misplaced?' Robin spluttered indignantly.

Cesare looked down his arrogant nose. 'It was not my intention to *ask* your father for anything, but to tell him when we are to be married!'

'Before you tell my father anything, don't you think you should actually ask me to marry you first?' Robin pointed out. 'Or is it that you think you have such an upper hand in this situation that my agreement is already a foregone conclusion?'

'And is it not?' Cesare drawled.

Robin could cheerfully have hit him at that moment, so deep was her frustrated anger at his autocratic attitude. And all, it seemed, because he had caught her coming out of Marco's nursery…

'Oh, I'm going to marry you, Cesare,' she assured him emotionally. 'If only to make your life the misery that you're making of mine!' She was breathing hard in her agitation.

Cesare watched the rapid rise and fall of her breasts, knowing they were unconfined beneath her dress; her legs and feet were bare too, telling him that she probably only wore the dress and panties. Two items of clothing he wanted to rip from her body before taking her with a savagery that was almost out of his control.

Almost.

Because he had never forced himself on any woman, and he did not intend to start with Robin.

No matter how she provoked him!

Besides, she had just conceded that she would marry him....

'I'm interested to know what you'll do if my father suggests we wait before getting married— get to know each other better before the question of marriage even arises,' Robin taunted.

'I am sure the fact that you stayed here with me last night will have told him we already know each other more than well enough for marriage,' he opined. 'Besides, I have every confidence that once you have reassured him of your feelings for me he will be happy to accept your decision.'

'My feelings for you, Cesare?' she parried.

He smiled humourlessly. 'You will, of course, *not* tell him that it is hate you feel for me rather than love!'

Did she hate this man? Robin wondered to herself. Could she possibly hate him and still find such pleasure in his arms, in his caresses?

Somehow she thought not…

Although Cesare might possibly grow to hate *her* once he realised that she wasn't about to produce the other Gambrelli sons and daughters he was obviously intending her to bear him.

She was saving that piece of information until after they were married and the shares in Ingram Publishing were safely back in her hands—she didn't dare risk Cesare learning she couldn't give him more children before she had those shares back! Though, after last night, she had another reason for maintaining her silence.

Marco…

She loved him—already couldn't bear the

thought of being parted from him if Cesare should discover her inability to give him more children and changed his mind about marrying her.

Maybe she was being a little unfair in not disclosing her apparent sterility to Cesare—but he wasn't exactly being fair, either, when he demanded that she marry him.

She gave a stiff inclination of her head. 'I'll tell my father that you will be coming to the house this evening.'

'Suitably assured of your own…desire for our marriage to take place, I hope?' Cesare demanded.

'Suitably assured of my determination that it will take place,' she corrected him. 'Believe me, if I could get those shares back any other way then I would,' she added untruthfully. The lure of becoming Marco's mother was more than enough to persuade her into marrying this man.

But she *really* couldn't risk Cesare even guessing that before they were safely married, those shares were back in her possession, and Marco was her stepson.

Cesare's mouth quirked. 'What a pity—for you—that there really is no other way…'

'You're the one to be pitied, Cesare—for wanting to marry a woman who doesn't love you,' Robin assured him heavily as he raised dark, questioning brows. 'Now, if you will excuse me, I have to go home and change before going to work— What is it *now,* Cesare?' She sighed wearily as he scowled down at her.

'You will cease to work for Ingram Publishing once we are married—'

'I most certainly will not!' she answered defiantly. 'My father needs me to remain close just now, Cesare.' She tried reasoning with him as he looked totally implacable.

'Marco and I will need you to remain close also,' he insisted.

'You and Marco have got along quite well without me so far. I'm sure you can continue to do so after we're married,' Robin dismissed.

She was so stubborn, this woman Cesare intended to make his wife. Beautiful, but stubborn. Desirable, but stubborn. Loyal to her family, but oh so stubborn!

'We will discuss this subject further once we are married,' he compromised tightly.

'We'll discuss it now!' Robin persisted. 'I've never been a stay-at-home wife. I wouldn't know how to be one.'

'You have your charity work—'

'It isn't enough, Cesare,' she said.

'You will have Marco—'

'Who, as you've already informed me, will continue to be cared for by the very capable Catriona!'

'Then I will find Catriona employment elsewhere!' Cesare told her exasperatedly, absolutely determined that Robin would *not* continue to work at Ingram Publishing after they were married.

He travelled extensively on business, and he intended that she and Marco would travel with him whenever he had to go away—something Robin would not be able to do if she were still working with her father.

As far as Cesare was concerned it was not even a subject for discussion.

Robin looked at him from beneath lowered lashes, wondering if Cesare had any idea that he had just given her exactly what she wanted—and that was to be able to care for Marco herself.

Of course Cesare had no idea—he wouldn't have made the suggestion if he had.

'Is that decision non-negotiable?' she prompted with false impatience.

'Absolutely,' he assured with certainty.

'Then it seems this is yet something else I have no choice about,' she conceded. 'Now, I really do have to go,' she finished, before turning to walk down the hallway to her bedroom to collect her things.

Robin was smiling as she closed the bedroom door behind her—a dreamy, ecstatic smile at the thought of taking care of her beloved Marco herself, all day every day.

In fact, she could almost love Cesare at that

moment for being the one to give her what she so wanted!

Love Cesare…?

No, she couldn't possibly feel love for such an arrogantly autocratic man, she told herself firmly.

Physical desire, yes.

But not love….

CHAPTER EIGHT

'CATRIONA HAS INFORMED me that she desires to return to Sicily once we return from our honeymoon.'

Robin frowned at Cesare later that evening, as he was shown into the sitting room of the home she had shared with her father for the last year. 'You've spoken to her already?'

'Actually…no,' he conceded ruefully. 'She was the one who spoke to me. Apparently her sister recently had a child, and she wishes to return to Sicily in order to care for her niece.'

'Did you say honeymoon?' Robin questioned, as part of his earlier comment registered. 'Who said anything about the two of us going away on a honeymoon?'

'It is traditional after a wedding, is it not?' he came back haughtily.

It might be, but theirs was hardly going to be a traditional wedding, was it?

She shook her head. 'I really don't think there's any need to carry the fiasco that far, Cesare—'

'Need or not, it will be expected,' Cesare maintained firmly.

Robin grimaced. 'By whom?'

'By your father, for one. I thought he would be here this evening...' Cesare frowned at the fact that her father was noticeably absent from the room.

It had been a long and trying day for Cesare so far, his business meetings having been more protracted than he would have wished. His thoughts had turned to Robin more often than he would have wished, too.

She looked wonderful again this evening, her cream dress perfect against the honey tones of her skin and the thick sheen of the long hair she wore loose about her shoulders. Her arms were bare, her legs long and silky in the stockings that Cesare now knew she favoured, instead of those unattractive tights most women wore, that he personally found so lacking in sensual allure.

Several times today he had found his mind wandering to thoughts of those long, long legs in their silk stockings, of the softness of her bare thighs above those sexy stocking-tops, of the silky triangle between her legs that he had so enjoyed caressing, of the taste of her as he'd suckled her nipples into the warmth of his mouth and brought her to shuddering release.

Thoughts that even now made his body harden with need!

So, yes, he intended taking Robin away on a honeymoon. He wanted to be alone with her somewhere for at least a week, so that they could explore every sensual pleasure together!

'Daddy had to go and take a telephone call in his study, but he should be back in a few minutes,' Robin excused. 'Would you care for a drink while we're waiting?' She indicated the array of spirits in cut-glass decanters on the side dresser.

What he would care for would be to put an end

to all of this and just be alone with Robin so that he could make love to her!

'A whisky will be fine,' he accepted instead, moving to sit down in one of the armchairs and watch Robin from between hooded lids as she deftly poured a measure of spirit for him.

Such long, sensual hands—hands that Cesare knew he wanted on his body with a need that made him impatient with everything and everyone else.

Once he got this necessary social meeting with her father out of the way, he intended taking Robin back to his hotel suite and taking her. And to hell with what the departing Catriona or anyone else thought!

Cesare seemed very distracted this evening, Robin noted, as she handed him the glass of whisky, finding his brooding silence unnerving.

'It was your idea to come here this evening, Cesare,' she reminded him dryly.

Those dark eyes glinted with impatience. 'I am not in the least concerned about your father's possible reaction to our plans for a hasty marriage, if that is what you are thinking, Robin.'

No, she wasn't thinking that at all. The shares that Cesare held in Ingram Publishing apart, he—with all his wealth and power—was not a man many people said no to.

Including herself, it seemed…

'I wouldn't feel too relaxed if I were you, Cesare,' she told him tartly, stung by his monumental self-confidence. 'A man's wealth is of little importance to my father when it comes to his suitability as a husband for his only daughter.'

Goodness knew, Giles had been wealthy enough—and look how disastrously that marriage had turned out!

'And you, Robin?' Cesare placed his untouched glass of whisky down on a side table before standing up, making her aware of his impeccably cut dark business suit, which was complemented by a white silk shirt and neatly knotted grey tie. 'What is important to you as regards suitability in a husband?' he encouraged, two long strides having brought him to stand directly in front of her.

Robin felt slightly overpowered by his proximity as she looked up into that darkly handsome face, and those black eyes were relentless as he easily held her gaze.

She swallowed hard. He was standing so close to her now she could feel the warmth of his body. She knew the power beneath that white silk shirt—had already touched and caressed his muscled strength yesterday.

She shook her head. 'The question hardly applies between us, does it, Cesare?' she responded.

'No?' He reached up to curve his hand about her throat, his thumb resting against the nerve pulsing in the hollow at its base.

'You are becoming aroused again, Robin,' he murmured with satisfaction.

'I—'

'Your pulse is racing.' He ignored her protest, his dark gaze heated on her parted lips as his thumb moved caressingly against her jaw. 'Your nipples are taut against your dress,' he observed approvingly, his eyes having lowered to her thrusting breasts before slowly returning to her mouth. 'You want me to kiss you,' he said, and his thumb moved to part her lips and his mouth took possession of hers.

She did want him to kiss her. Robin couldn't deny it, even as her body curved into his, her arms moving up about his shoulders and her fingers becoming entangled in the dark thickness of his hair.

She had no explanation for the madness she knew in this man's arms—no will to fight it either, as Cesare slowly drew her bottom lip into his mouth, his tongue caressing its inner sensitivity as warmth spread through her whole body. Her groan was one of hunger as his tongue thrust fully into her mouth.

'Perhaps I should come back later…?'

Robin wrenched her mouth from Cesare's at the first sound of her father's voice, giving Cesare a slightly accusing look as she wondered if he hadn't kissed her with the sole intention of being caught in the act.

She turned away from his unreadable expression. 'Don't be silly, Daddy,' she dismissed teasingly as she crossed the room to her father on legs that shook slightly, linking her arm with his and drawing him farther into the room. 'I don't need to introduce the two of you, do I?' she asked lightly.

'Gambrelli,' her father said curtly, and he held out his hand.

'Ingram,' Cesare answered just as curtly, as he briefly shook the older man's hand, impatient with the interruption—although in truth, holding Robin in his arms, kissing her, he had forgotten that her father was expected to make an appearance, had forgotten where they were!

Robin gave a husky laugh. 'Now, I want the two of you to return to your corners and when the bell goes come out fighting!'

Charles Ingram ignored her levity as his stare remained locked on Cesare's.

It was a silent battle of wills, Cesare acknowledged, with grudging admiration for this man who was Robin's father.

But he had also been the father of Simon

Ingram—the man Cesare held responsible for Carla's death!

His mouth hardened. 'I do not think your father appreciates your humour, Robin,' he reproved tersely.

'And you?' She looked up to taunt him. 'Do *you* appreciate my humour, Cesare?'

He gave Charles Ingram one last narrow-eyed look before turning his attention to Robin, deliberately softening his expression as he saw the light of challenge in her eyes, her cheeks slightly flushed. With temper rather than arousal, he thought.

He smiled slightly. 'I, of course, appreciate everything about you, Robin,' he drawled mockingly.

That flush deepened in her cheeks. 'Well, of course you do,' she replied stiffly. 'Daddy, Cesare has come here this evening so that we can all sit down cosily together and discuss our wedding plans,' she explained. 'When is the wedding to be, Cesare?' she prompted, her voice brittle.

Cesare saw the way Charles Ingram's frown

deepened, knowing as he did so that Robin was coming perilously close to revealing the tension between the two of them. It did not bother him personally, but he had thought the pretence important to Robin.

What had he done to anger Robin so much that she was in danger of revealing the disharmony between them when she had already assured him she wanted to keep it from her father?

'That is, of course, for you to decide, Robin,' he replied smoothly.

'Is it?' she scorned, with that same recklessness.

Cesare's mouth tightened. 'As long as it is within the next few weeks, yes.'

'The next few *weeks?*' Charles Ingram was the one to exclaim as he turned to look at his daughter incredulously.

Cesare gave an abrupt inclination of his head.

That was news to Robin. But why should it be? Cesare had told her this morning that he was tired of the delay...

She was filled with conflicting emotions at the

thought of them being married so soon. Positive feelings because it seemed she was to become Marco's mother in a matter of days. And uncertainty because it also meant she would become Cesare's wife at the same time—a wife he had nothing but contempt for.

Well…that wasn't quite true. Cesare obviously felt desire for her too.

As she desired him…

But at the moment she was angry with him for what she perceived as his manipulation of her physical response to him just now—timed so that her father had walked in on the two of them obviously in a passionate clinch. She didn't at all like the way Cesare had used her response to him against her.

'This is preposterous,' her father exclaimed. 'The two of you have known each other only a matter of days—'

'Sometimes that is all it takes,' Cesare answered him quietly.

'Robin…?' Her father appealed to her agitatedly.

Her heart ached at the bewilderment she could

see in his face. She knew that he was concerned for her, but at the same time was aware there was little she could say that would alleviate his concern. Not without telling him the truth. And she had no intention of doing that.

'Sometimes that's all it takes, Daddy.' She sadly repeated Cesare's words.

'But—'

'I understand your concerns, Charles,' Cesare told the older man smoothly. 'But Robin is a grown woman—certainly old enough to make her own decisions about her future.'

'And her own mistakes,' her father came back impatiently.

Robin's breath caught in her throat as she saw the way Cesare stiffened and looked down his arrogant nose at her father. It instantly brought her back to an awareness that Cesare was only playing this role for her sake—that he actually cared nothing at all for either her own or her father's feelings.

'My marrying Cesare won't be a mistake, Daddy,' she assured her parent as she removed her arm from linking with his and moved to stand at Cesare's side. But not quite touching him… 'We love each other. We want to get married as soon as possible. And we— I would like your blessing.' She looked at her father with the same appeal he had used on her seconds ago.

'But whether you give us your blessing or not, we still intend to be married,' Cesare stated implacably.

Robin gave him a quick glance, knowing by the pulse she could see beating in his tightly clenched jaw that Cesare was very close to losing the temper he usually kept under such rigid control.

And that she had probably helped push him there with her slightly reckless behaviour a few minutes ago.

But she resented being manipulated like this!

Which was slightly ridiculous of her when Cesare had done nothing *but* manipulate her, from the moment he'd come here two days ago and told her of his demands!

'Then it seems I have little choice, doesn't it?' Her father sighed wearily. 'If this is really what

Robin wants, then of course I wish you every happiness together.'

Robin's sadness for her father grew at the same time as she acknowledged there was nothing she could say or do that would alleviate his anxiety. The truth—that Simon had gambled away his shares in Ingram Publishing—would hurt her father so much more than this apparently impetuous marriage of hers could ever do.

'It's what I want, Daddy,' she assured him quietly.

Cesare found himself brooding as he listened to the conversation between father and daughter.

Although why he should be in the least disturbed, he had no idea. Hadn't he already used the deep love that existed between father and daughter in order to force Robin into marrying him?

Yes, of course he had. He just hadn't expected to feel quite so…discomforted at being the cause of this obvious tension between Robin and her father…

'I'll ring for Cameron and have him bring some champagne—'

'I am afraid Robin and I have a previous engagement.' Cesare cut abruptly across the other man's suggestion, feeling Robin's surprised gaze on him as he kept his attention firmly fixed on Charles Ingram. 'As I am sure you appreciate, we still have much to discuss,' he added, with a slightest softening of his tone.

'Of course,' Charles acknowledged heavily. 'I— Will you be back tonight, Robin?' he asked politely.

'I—'

'No, she will not,' Cesare replied firmly.

'I see.' Charles's face only sagged further at this news. 'In that case I'll talk to you tomorrow, Robin,' he told her gently.

It did not take two guesses on Cesare's part to know exactly what the other man wished to talk to Robin about.

'Did you have to be so…so bloody-minded?' Robin attacked as soon as the two of them were seated in Cesare's car—a sleek black sports car of a make Robin had only previously seen in exclusive showrooms.

Cesare shrugged unconcernedly. 'I saw little point in giving your father the impression there was any room for uncertainty about the timing of our forthcoming marriage.'

No, he wouldn't, Robin realised resentfully. Her poor father, on the other hand, had still looked totally bewildered when they'd left, obviously completely dazed by the speed with which they had decided to spend the rest of their lives together.

Oh, God…

Her heart sank, and the palms of her hands were suddenly damp just at the thought of marrying Cesare, let alone spending the rest of her life with him. He was so completely unlike Giles, whose manners and consideration for others had been impeccable—to the point that he had even asked her permission before they made love. Quite an annoying trait, actually, but a little less arrogance on Cesare's part might be nice.

Nice?

What a ridiculous word to even think of in connection with Cesare!

She sighed heavily, relaxing back in her seat, knowing there was no point in even pursuing the subject of his behaviour towards her father. 'Exactly what is this previous engagement you mentioned to my father?' she prompted irritably.

Cesare didn't answer, merely gave her a glance from eyes that gleamed black in the semi-darkness of the lamp-lit street. But it was the sort of glance that brought warm colour to Robin's cheeks and set her pulse racing erratically.

She swallowed hard. The intent in his dark eyes was unmistakable. 'I thought you considered it inappropriate for us to share a bedroom while we're unmarried and Marco's nursemaid is still in residence?' she reminded him, slightly breathless.

Cesare seemed unperturbed. 'I have decided that I no longer care about Catriona's sensibilities,' he responded levelly, his hands tightly gripping the steering wheel.

'And if I do?'

'You will have to overcome them!' Cesare

rasped. His time of self-denial was at an end. He wanted Robin—wanted her with a need that made his body scream.

She gave him a scathing glance. 'And what if I'm not in the mood to play the acquiescent woman?'

She was deliberately trying to bring about an argument between them again, Cesare knew. Unfortunately, she had chosen completely the wrong way in which to do it.

He gave a humourless smile. 'Acquiescence is the last thing I want from you, Robin. In fact, I would much rather that you kicked and yelled—the latter in ecstasy, of course,' he added dryly.

'Surely that depends on where I decide to kick you?' she came back, undaunted.

Cesare's smile deepened into appreciation. Acquiescent woman, hah! That was one thing Robin would never be—and the last thing that he wanted her to be.

'There are many ways for a man and woman to find pleasure together, Robin,' he reminded her, knowing he had made his point when, after a resentful glare in his direction, she turned her face to look firmly out of the passenger window.

Her efforts to ignore him were spoilt slightly, however, by the rapid rise and fall of those pert breasts, and the less than steady sound of her breathing.

Cesare continued to smile as he put his foot down on the accelerator, his anticipation growing by the second, and increasing rapidly once he had parked his car in the underground car park beneath the Gambrelli Hotel. The sexual tension between them was so intense by the time he moved round the car to open Robin's door for her that Cesare knew he could wait no longer—that he had to at least taste her now.

His mouth claimed hers.

It was no gentle kiss, but Robin's lips instantly parted beneath the onslaught of his, her body pressed hard against him as her fingers became entangled in his hair and she returned his kiss with a hunger that made his control slip dangerously low.

Cesare pressed her back against the car as he

deepened the kiss. Tongues battled briefly before he plundered the moist cavern of her mouth in the same rhythm as his hips thrust against hers, slowly, surely, until he felt he would burst with his need to be inside her.

He continued to kiss her as he pushed her dress up about her waist, pushed her panties aside, his fingers seeking to caress her, touching her moisture, feeling her readiness for him even as he found the centre of her pleasure and began to stroke her, driving his body against her as he felt the spasms that began to shake her body.

Robin wrenched her mouth from his. 'Not here, Cesare!' she breathed, her body trembling with arousal. 'We can't make love here,' she protested weakly.

Cesare looked down at her, his eyes black, a sensual flush to his high cheekbones. 'I want you now, Robin. I am not sure I can wait until we reach my suite!' he told her shakily, the hardness of his thighs still pressed throbbingly against her.

Robin could feel Cesare's urgency, knew that same throbbing need herself, wanting to tear the

clothes from his body and have him take her—
right here, right now.

'Don't you understand? I want to make love to
you too, Cesare!' she groaned. This was so much
more intense than the last time they had made
love; Robin was being driven wild with wanting
him. 'I want to touch and caress you in the same
way you're touching and caressing me. I want—
I want it all, Cesare!' she told him passionately.

His hands—subtle, sensuous hands that knew
how to caress her to wild abandon—moved up to
cradle each side of her face and he looked down
at her searchingly. 'Then you shall, Robin,' he finally murmured gruffly, before taking her hand
firmly in his as he marched over to key in his
personal code for the private lift.

The two of them stepped inside. Robin was
aware of their sexual tension heightening to an
impossible level as they waited impatiently for
the lift to stop at the penthouse suite, their earlier
discord totally forgotten in that need.

'I am yours,' Cesare promised, as they stepped
out of the lift, maintaining that hold on her hand

as he strode forcefully down the hallway to his bedroom and closed the door behind them, raising dark brows as Robin switched on the light.

'I want to look at you,' she explained huskily, her fingers shaking in anticipation as she slipped his jacket from his shoulders and unbuttoned his shirt, to strip that from his body too and throw it down on the carpet beside his jacket. 'All of you,' she added intensely, as she unzipped his trousers and drew them down the long length of his legs.

She had never undressed a man before, and never delighted in each new discovery. Cesare's legs were long and muscled, covered with the same dark hair that lay on his bared chest and then went down in a vee into his fitted underpants. These she also drew down and discarded, releasing his manhood to her caressing gaze as she knelt in front of him.

A caress that her hands quickly followed, touching him there, and she watched the way his body leapt in reponse before she moved to trail her tongue moistly down that hard shaft, encouraged to deeper intimacies as Cesare gasped breathlessly and his hands became entangled in her hair.

Robin relished the feel and taste of him, relished the way Cesare couldn't hide his response to her caresses. His breathing was ragged as he reached down suddenly to draw her to her feet.

'I want to be inside you!' Cesare groaned, even as he deftly dealt with the zip on her dress, dropping the garment to the carpet, his eyes darkening to jet as he looked at the firm thrust of her bared breasts. Her creamy lacy panties and those oh-so-delectable stockings were her only clothing now.

He lowered his head to capture one of those pouting nipples with the heated warmth of his mouth, his tongue a rasp as he suckled, knowing by the way Robin trembled that she was as aroused as he was.

'You are so beautiful, Robin,' he breathed as he raised his head to look down at her, his body pulsating with the need to be inside her. 'I am afraid I cannot be gentle this first time!' He shook his head as he stripped the cream lace from her body.

'Next time I will go slower,' he promised, even as he laid her down on the bed and moved between her parted thighs. 'Next time we will both go slower!' he groaned, as her thighs moved up to meet his, and with a single thrust Robin took him deep inside her.

Even as Cesare fiercely claimed her mouth with his, he knew he had never experienced pleasure like this, never wanted a woman in the way that he did Robin.

She took him deeper inside her with each thrust. Minutes later he could feel the release building inside him, knew it was too urgent to be controlled. Robin's back was arching in the same need as he wrenched his mouth from hers to suckle hungrily on her breast and draw it deep inside his mouth, and her nails were digging into his back as her cries of release matched his. Their pleasure exploded into a kaleidescope of feelings and emotions, of pleasure that seemed never-ending.

Robin felt dazed and wondrous as she lay beneath him, her hands moving caressingly across the damp width of his back even as she acknowledged that this lovemaking with Cesare was beyond anything she had ever known before— that never in her years of marriage had she ever reached a wild and uncontrollable climax like the one she and Cesare had just shared together.

She didn't understand what it meant…

Did it mean that she was a more physical person than she had ever dreamt possible?

Or had this been so different because she had feelings for Cesare?

Because she might even have fallen in love with him…?

CHAPTER NINE

'WHAT IS IT?' Cesare lifted his head to look down at Robin as he sensed her mental withdrawal from him. 'Robin, tell me what is wrong?' he prompted, lifting his weight from her to lie down beside her and look down at her searchingly.

'Wrong?' she echoed emotionally. 'What could possibly be wrong?' she choked. 'I've just— we've just ripped each other's clothes off and taken each other like two—'

'Do not do this to yourself, Robin,' Cesare silenced her, his expression dark as he saw exactly where she was going with this conversation. 'We wanted each other—'

'Exactly!' she cried, turning away from him to move to the edge of the bed and sit up. 'I don't know myself like this!' she groaned as she buried her face in her hands.

'Robin…' Cesare reached out a hand to touch her creamy back.

She stiffened beneath his touch. 'Please don't!' she instructed shakily, standing up to move away from him, unknowingly arousing in those silk stockings she still wore. 'I have to go.' She shook her head. 'I need to go!' she said determinedly, and she bent down to pick up her dress.

Cesare moved swiftly, stilling her movements as she attempted to pull the dress back on. 'And I need you to stay,' he told her huskily, his gaze intent on hers as she looked up at him uncertainly. 'I very much need you to stay, Robin…' he repeated gently. 'If only to show you that just now was only one of the many ways in which we will find happiness together.'

She should never have looked at him, Robin knew. Should never have felt herself drowning in those coal-black eyes. Should never have looked at that sensuous mouth that could give such pleasure. Certainly should never have swayed towards him in mute appeal, the hunger of her kiss exactly matching his!

Because she *did* know herself in that moment—only too well. Realised that somehow, in the days since she'd first met him, she had fallen in love with Cesare.

And it was a love that made her completely unable to say no to him as he began to caress the curves of her body once again, reawakening her earlier need. But it was a need he had no intention of satisfying just yet. Once again he laid her down on the bed. His lips followed the same caressing path as his hands, gently rolling the silk stockings down her legs, and kissed the soles of her feet in a surprisingly erotic caress that made Robin's toes curl.

Cesare chuckled softly as he moved up her body to kiss the two rosy peaks of her breasts, before suckling them slowly, his tongue a rasp against their sensitivity, then releasing them to move his lips and tongue down the taut flatness of her stomach. He lingered at her navel as he moistly caressed that hollow, and his hand moved lower, parting the silky hair to stroke her already sensitised nub.

Robin's body arched in pleasure, her groans pleading now, sounds Cesare moved to satisfy as his lips and tongue replaced caressing fingers and he tasted and teased and filled her with an aching warmth that spread from her abdomen to the thighs she parted to allow his deeper caress.

'I can't,' she gasped. 'I really can't—'

'Oh, yes—you really can,' Cesare assured her, and he flicked his tongue against her and watched as she blossomed and flowered beneath his caress. 'I want to give you every pleasure there is, Robin,' he whispered. 'Want to touch you until I know your body intimately!' he added. His tongue plunged into her and he felt her spasm with a release that made her cry out. Her hands tangled in the thickness of his hair and she held him to her so that she might drink in every last moment of that release.

Cesare entered and filled her while her climax still tremored through her body, feeling those inner waves as she took and held him, his movements slow and measured as he felt the pleasure slowly building in her once again. He held back from reaching his own peak until he knew she was ready to join him, his gaze holding hers as they reached the pinnacle together.

'Sleep now,' Cesare breathed minutes later, when he was able to speak again. 'Sleep, Robin, and we will talk in the morning,' he assured her. And his arms tightened about her as he lay beside her, anchoring her to his side.

Robin had no idea how long she had slept with her head resting on Cesare's shoulder. She woke up to find the space beside her in he bed empty and sunlight streaming in through the window.

She stretched slowly, her body aching slightly— a pleasurable sensation caused by the strength of Cesare's hands and mouth. Just the thought of the intimacy of his touch brought the warmth of colour to her cheeks.

Cheeks that just as quickly paled as she remembered her newly realised feelings for Cesare. She was in love with him. Was in love with the man who was forcing her to marry him. Was in love with the man who didn't need to use any force at all when he made love to her so beautifully...

What was she going to do?

How could she possibly marry Cesare knowing that she was in love with him, but that his only feelings for her were sexual attraction and a need for revenge on her family?

What choice did she have? she realised hopelessly. Cesare had given her no choice. Was giving her no choice—

'What are you thinking now?' Cesare asked as he came through from the adjoining bathroom, completely unconcerned by his nakedness.

Deservedly so, Robin acknowledged as she looked at him from beneath lowered lashes; Cesare had the most beautiful male body she had ever seen!

She really couldn't tell him what she was thinking at that moment—was shocked at the wantonness of her own thoughts.

Her eyes moved swiftly back to his face as he moved to stretch out on the bed beside her, trapping her beneath the duvet as he rolled over to look down at her.

'I was thinking that it's time for me to leave—' she said.

'Not before breakfast, surely?' he interrupted her indulgently.

She shook her head. 'I couldn't eat a thing.'

'Food is not on the menu,' he assured her huskily, and he parted the softness of her lips with one sensuous finger.

Robin swallowed hard, wanting to moisten her suddenly dry lips, but knowing that the movement would bring her tongue into contact with his finger in an act of pure intimacy.

'It isn't my intention to have the honeymoon before the wedding, Cesare!' She forced her tone to be ascerbic as she moved determinedly away from him, sliding sideways so that she could get out of bed.

A mistake on her part. She realised she was as naked as Cesare, and in no position to attempt the dignified exit she had planned on making!

Cesare lay back on the bed, his hands upon

the pillow behind his head, as he watched Robin move about the room collecting up her scattered clothing.

She really was an enigma, this woman who was to be his wife: initially a wildcat in his arms last night, followed by that long, slow loving, and now, this morning, it seemed as if she was embarrassed by the intensity of their lovemaking.

Could it really be that she had been telling the truth when she'd told him she had only had one lover, her first husband, before him…?

He found it incredible, if it were true; Robin was a beautiful and sensual woman, with a capacity for physical pleasure he had never encountered with any other woman.

He smiled at the thought of the years they were going to have together.

'Would you like to share whatever it is you find so funny?' she snapped as she saw—and misinterpreted—that smile. Her face was flushed with emotion as she glared down at him, once again wearing her cream dress, although she still held her panties and stockings in her hand.

Cesare shook his head. 'That was a smile of satisfaction, Robin, not humour,' he drawled.

If anything her blush deepened. 'A smug smile of satisfaction, no doubt!' she retorted.

His good humour faded. 'Why do you persist in deliberately provoking an argument between the two of us every time we come anywhere near an understanding of each other?' he bit out impatiently as he threw back the duvet to get out of bed.

'Understanding of each other?' Robin repeated, wishing he would put some clothes on instead of standing there looking so magnificently naked—and at the same time evoking memories she would rather forget! 'I could never come to an understanding with *any* man who uses force on a woman!' she riposted, eyes sparkling deeply purple.

His mouth tightened. 'I did not force you last night, Robin,' he replied stiffly. 'As I recall, you were the one who could not wait to take my clothes off as soon as we entered the bedroom!'

'I meant force a woman into marrying you!'

Robin corrected frustratedly, knowing she had walked straight into that one.

'You—' Cesare broke off as a knock sounded on the bedroom door. 'Yes?' he prompted tersely.

'You have a telephone call, Signor Gambrelli.' Catriona, Marco's nursemaid, sounded hesitant—probably because she had heard the sound of a female voice in her employer's bedroom, Robin acknowledged with a wince. 'I would not have disturbed you, Signor, but he said to tell you it is Count Gambrelli,' the girl added awkwardly.

'Count Gambrelli?' Robin echoed frowningly.

'My cousin,' Cesare explained impatiently, before answering the nanny. 'Tell him I will be there in a moment,' he called out as he began to pull clean clothes from the wardrobe.

'Count Gambrelli?' Robin said again, having received a clear impression from Cesare that he and his sister Carla were the last of the Gambrelli family.

Cesare shot her an impatient glance as he pulled on his clothes. 'I am only half-Sicilian on my mother's side. My father was Italian. He was the younger and disinherited brother of the previous Count Gambrelli,' he grated. 'Disinherited because he married a woman his family did not consider suitable,' he elaborated, as he straightened, fully dressed now, and ran his fingers through the dark length of his hair before turning to leave. 'Do not go before I return,' he paused to tell her before opening the door.

Robin eyed him mockingly. 'Perhaps this… titled connection explains some of your own arrogance…' she concluded.

Cesare gave her a fierce glance before leaving the bedroom and closing the door firmly behind him.

Robin's smile faded as she moved through to the adjoining bathroom to finish dressing, running a brush quickly through her tangled hair as she heard Cesare return to the bedroom. She was thankful, when she checked her reflection in the full-length mirror, that she once again looked the composed Robin Ingram she had always been before Cesare had entered her life.

Cesare was still scowling when she walked back into the bedroom. 'My cousin—'

'The count?' she put in derisively.

'My cousin,' he repeated, eyes narrowed warningly, 'is a guest in the hotel, and has called to see if it is convenient for him to join me for breakfast.'

A suggestion that had obviously got him rattled. 'And is it?' Robin questioned, an eyebrow raised.

Cesare's agitation seemed to deepen. 'I could not think of any reason why it is not!' he admitted frustratedly.

Robin smiled at his obvious discomfort. 'Don't worry, Cesare, I'll leave before he gets here and so save your reputation from certain ruin!'

She was no more eager to meet his cousin, this Count Gambrelli, under these circumstances than Cesare obviously was for her to do so!

Although she had hoped to see something of Marco again this morning before she left. But that obviously wasn't going to happen unless she actually asked to see him. Something she dared not do.

Cesare's mouth twisted derisively. 'That will not be possible, I am afraid. I have already informed Wolf that my fiancée is here, too.'

'Wolf...?' Robin repeated incredulously. 'Where on earth did he get such a— Your fiancée, Cesare...?' She looked at him uncertainly.

'That is what you are, is it not?' Cesare stated flatly, feeling far from pleased at this unexpected visit from the cousin he had not seen for months.

Despite being of similar ages, the two men were far from close; in fact they had never even met each other until a couple of years ago, when Wolf's father had died and he'd inherited the title and decided that past rifts in the family were none of his affair.

Besides, Wolf was also one of the biggest playboys in Europe.

And Robin was one of the most beautiful women...

Jealousy was not something that had ever been part of Cesare's nature—he had never cared enough for any woman to be concerned or otherwise about her fidelity. But Robin was different. She was about to become his wife—and, as he was painfully aware, the oh-so-charming Wolf was not the one forcing Robin into marriage!

'A fiancée usually wears a ring, Cesare,' Robin told him. 'And, no, I'm not angling for you to present me with one,' she added quickly, before he could even make such a suggestion. 'Our...arrangement doesn't require an engagement ring.'

'Nevertheless, I intend introducing you to Wolf as my betrothed,' Cesare stated. 'He is very much looking forward to meeting you.'

'Then I'm afraid he's going to be disappointed,' Robin returned. 'This really isn't the right time for me to meet any of your family, Cesare.'

'I am sure you will find Wolf very charming,' he came back.

'Now, wouldn't that be a novelty in a Gambrelli?' she said archly. 'Perhaps I should stay and meet him after all.'

Cesare's eyes narrowed. 'Do not try my patience too far, Robin, by even attempting to—'

'What patience is that, Cesare?' she responded ruefully. 'I've certainly never seen any! Not tolerance, either,' she added. 'But then, I suppose, when you're perfect yourself, you don't have time for other people's mistakes!'

Cesare had no doubt she was referring to her brother's mistakes, but it was a subject that Cesare had no intention of talking about yet again.

'I do not consider myself perfect, Robin,' he replied. 'Far from it, in fact!'

Luckily—or unluckily!—the bell to his suite rang, announcing Wolf's arrival, before Robin could make any comment on that claim.

'You must at least say good morning to Wolf before you are able to leave,' Cesare ordered as he moved to the bedroom door. 'Come, I will introduce the two of you.'

Robin waited in the sitting room while Cesare went to open the door for his cousin, hearing the rich timbre of their voices as they greeted each other. Her eyes widened in surprise as she looked at the tall and handsome man dressed in a casual shirt and fitted trousers who followed Cesare into the room.

Looking at the two men together was like seeing a black and white negative next to a photograph: Wolf's hair was a rich honey mane in comparison to the almost-black of Cesare's, but the dark brown eyes were the same, and there was quite a similarity in their looks and build too. Count Wolf Gambrelli was just as devastatingly good-looking as Cesare!

'Miss Ingram—or may I call you Robin, as it seems you are about to become my cousin-in-law?' the Count greeted her in smoothly accentless English, those brown eyes warm with appreciation as he moved to kiss her warmly on both cheeks.

Closely watched by a scowling Cesare, Robin noted as she distractedly returned the other man's greeting. 'Of course,' she agreed lightly. 'Although unfortunately I can't stay to enjoy breakfast with the two of you,' she explained briskly, more than ever determined to make good her escape now that she had actually met Wolf—

two devastatingly handsome Gambrelli men was definitely two too many! 'I'm afraid I have to get off to work now.' She smiled her apology.

'What a pity,' Wolf Gambrelli murmured softly, and he continued to look at her admiringly.

'Is it not?' Cesare was the one to speak as he took a firm grip of Robin's arm with the intention of walking her to the lift. 'I will return momentarily, Wolf,' he threw over his shoulder.

'Take as long as you want,' his cousin dismissed languidly as he lowered his long, elegant length into one of the armchairs. 'I am sure that if I were engaged to Robin I would not wish to hurry my goodbye, either,' he opined with lazy charm.

Whew. Robin breathed hard once she and Cesare were outside in the hallway; Wolf Gambrelli, despite her initial surprise at his unusual first name, definitely lived up to it!

'You could certainly take a few lessons in charm from your cousin, Cesare,' she told him mockingly.

'Wolf has a mistress in Paris and another in Milan,' Cesare countered.

Robin studied him with a frown. If she hadn't known better, she would have said that Cesare was jealous of the attention his handsome cousin had shown her. But as she did know better...

Besides, Cesare might not be aware of it—please goodness he wasn't aware of it!—but she was in love with him. Deeply. Irrevocably.

'Then there's probably room for a third in London,' she came back smartly, instantly rewarded for her brittle humour by the tightening of Cesare's fingers on her arm. 'You're hurting me, Cesare,' she told him.

'I will do more than hurt you if you ever go near my rake of a cousin without my knowledge!' he warned between gritted teeth.

Her brows rose. 'Believe me, Cesare, one Gambrelli man in my life is already one too many!'

His eyes glittered as he looked down at her, a nerve pulsing in his tightly clenched jaw. 'You did not seem to think so last night,' he reminded her smoothly.

Robin felt the warmth in her body. 'How typical of a man to taunt a moment of physical weakness!' she retorted, and she tried to pull away from his grasp on her arm.

But she didn't succeed. Cesare pulled her in close against the hardness of his body. 'I did not mean to—' He broke off. 'I was no more able to deny what happened between us last night than you were.' His voice softened. 'What would have happened again this morning if we had not been interrupted,' he acknowledged.

Robin knew it was true—that if his cousin hadn't turned up, their argument would once again have resulted in the two of them making love, that when she was in Cesare's arms she had no thought of denial.

She avoided his gaze. 'You really should get back to your cousin,' she said stiltedly.

'I drove you here last night, so how do you intend to get home?' He frowned as the thought seemed to occur to him.

Robin shrugged unconcernedly. 'This is a hotel. I'm sure there are plenty of taxis downstairs.'

Cesare shook his head. 'By the time you get downstairs a courtesy car will be waiting at the hotel entrance to drive you back to your home.'

Of course it would, Robin accepted. No doubt once she was Cesare's wife she would learn to take this super-luxurious lifestyle of Cesare's for granted. Maybe…

She nodded. 'I really do have to go.'

'Not until I have kissed you…' Cesare groaned as his head lowered and his mouth once more took possession of hers, blocking all thought, all emotion, other than the ones he aroused.

Robin was completely unresisting by the time Cesare raised his head to look down at her.

'I will call you later and we will arrange to spend the evening and the night together,' he told her.

Robin breathed raggedly. 'A please might be nice,' she murmured ruefully.

Cesare gave a relaxed smile, totally reassured of just how much she desired him by Robin's un-inhibited response. 'I will endeavour to do more than *please* you later this evening,' he promised softly, and was rewarded with that becoming blush to her cheeks.

Robin, he had discovered, when he had woken this morning and just lain looking at her for several long minutes as she slept, was one of those women who looked just as beautiful without make-up as she did with it, her complexion naturally creamy, her lips a pouting rose.

'In fact,' he went on, 'I will look forward to it!' He kissed her once more, lingeringly, savouring the taste of her, before he released her. 'Until this evening...' His tone promised more—much more.

Cesare stood and watched Robin as she got into the lift, waiting until she had pressed the button for the lobby and the lift doors had closed behind her before he turned to go back to the sitting room, where his cousin was waiting to have breakfast with him.

CHAPTER TEN

'I REALLY DON'T understand why this conversation couldn't have waited until this evening, Cesare.' Robin addressed him across the width of her desk a couple of hours later, where he stood so tall and powerful in the confines of her office on the executive floor of Ingram Publishing.

She had thought that at least her place of work was safe from his invasion—but, having received a phone call from him a short time ago to say he was coming to see her immediately, she had accepted that even her office would now be filled with memories of him!

Cesare was wearing a dark brown business suit, teamed with a cream shirt and a brown tie, and he looked dark and distant—completely unlike the naked lover she had left earlier this morning.

Thank goodness! Her office was the last place

in which she wanted to succumb to the desire she felt every time she so much as looked at him!

Somehow, in the last twenty-four hours, she had lost sight of the reason she was marrying Cesare—the reason she was being forced to marry him!

Her physical response to him was blocking every other emotion from her mind.

To the point that she had allowed herself to fall in love with him!

But it was a love that Cesare didn't feel for her—that he would never feel for her. She would be a fool to allow that emotion to rule her head as well as her heart.

Although, with Cesare in this arrogantly distant mood, there was little danger of that happening at the moment!

'It could not wait because I will not be here this evening,' he told her, as he paced her office with the restlessness of a caged tiger.

Robin watched him carefully. 'Then where will you be?'

'The where is not important,' he told her

brusquely. 'I merely wanted you to understand that I have to go away on business. *Immediately,*' he added, brooking no argument.

She gave a slightly dazed shake of her head. 'Couldn't you have told me when you called earlier, and saved yourself the trouble of coming here?'

Cesare eyed her frustratedly, not liking the image she presented as she sat behind her executive desk, dressed in a tailored black suit and oh-so-prim cream blouse, her hair once more confined in that neat chignon—looking absolutely nothing like the warm, desirable woman who had shared his bed the night before!

'I thought it better to come here and explain my departure to you in person,' he replied. 'So that there can be no…misunderstandings between us.'

She sat straighter behind the desk, a telltale blush to her cheeks. 'But as usual you aren't explaining, Cesare, only telling.' She sighed. 'Does this abrupt departure have anything to do with your cousin's visit this morning?'

Cesare's eyes narrowed as he looked at her.

'And why should you think that?' he prompted guardedly.

'For goodness' sake, Cesare.' Robin snapped her impatience at his suspicious tone. 'It's barely two hours since we parted, and yet you've suddenly decided to go away on business—surely it's only logical to think that Wolf—Count Gambrelli,' she corrected as Cesare scowled, 'might in some way be responsible for your sudden decision to leave London?'

Logical, perhaps. Correct, even. But Cesare did not yet intend discussing with Robin the reason for his sudden announcement. He might find himself on a wild-goose chase.

And if he did not, then he would have plenty of explaining to do to Robin when he returned…

'Perhaps,' he allowed. 'But I do not expect to be gone long. Perhaps only twenty-four hours.'

Twenty-four hours too long, as far as Cesare was concerned. Although Robin's comment that he might have told her that he was going away when he'd called earlier seemed to imply there wasn't the same reluctance on *her* part at the thought of their parting!

And why should there be? They had found a physical perfection together last night that Cesare had never known before with any woman. But, for Robin, that would not detract from the fact that he was forcing her to marry him.

'I see,' she said slowly. 'Would you like me to go to your suite later and check that Catriona and Marco are okay?' she offered lightly.

Lightly, because Robin still didn't dare let Cesare know how eager she was to see the baby again—to hold him, to hear his lovely chuckle as she tickled his neck.

Nevertheless, Cesare's eyes widened in surprise at her suggestion. 'I would not like to put you to that trouble—'

'Oh, it's no trouble,' Robin assured him. 'I think I left my earrings in your bathroom anyway, so I can pick them up at the same time.'

'If you are sure...?'

'Why not?' Robin returned, avoiding meeting his eyes as she straightened some papers on her desk. 'It's just as easy for me to go that way home.'

He nodded. 'I will telephone Catriona and tell her to expect you.'

'If you think it necessary, Cesare,' Robin retorted. 'But I'm hardly likely to kidnap Marco, now, am I?' she went on, knowing that Cesare still believed her to be not keen to have children.

'I should go now,' Cesare said, at the same time making no effort to leave as he continued to look at her with those dark, enigmatic eyes.

'Yes,' Robin acknowledged huskily, held immobile by his dark brown gaze.

'My private plane is already fuelled and waiting to leave,' he said finally, breaking the spell.

His private plane? Yes, of course Cesare would have his own jet. As he had his own penthouse suite in all his hotels all over the world—and no doubt a car waiting for him in every international capital too. Probably a home in Sicily, as well— a huge, luxurious villa that he would return to whenever he could.

'I will call you while I am away,' he promised.

'That will be nice.' Robin gave an uncertain smile, wondering why he didn't just leave and get this parting over with.

What was the saying? Something like the sooner he left the sooner he would be back? As she felt the pain of their parting, she was already looking forward to his return.

He really did have to leave now, Cesare knew, and yet a part of him was loath to go, to leave Robin when they were only tentatively coming to an understanding of each other—

No!

He should be honest with himself, at least. After making love with Robin, holding her in his arms all night long, he was the one who didn't want to be parted from her.

'Come with me,' he invited impulsively, and then inwardly chided himself. He knew that taking Robin with him would not be a good idea—that she would be too much of a distraction, and that what he had to do he had to do alone.

'I don't think that's a good idea, do you?' she refused quickly. 'No,' she went on, when she clearly saw the doubt in his expression. 'I really do have some work I have to be getting on with now, Cesare…'

His mouth firmed at her dismissal. 'It is customary in my country to kiss a fiancé goodbye,' he grated, not meaning to sound so harsh, but unable to control the emotion.

Robin gave a rueful smile. 'I think we've already had the fiancé conversation once today, Cesare!'

'And I'm sure we will have it many more times before we are married!' he rejoined, moving around the desk to pull her to her feet and take her in his arms. 'Perhaps you might even find you miss me a little while I am away…?' he murmured questioningly.

A little? Robin missed him already—and he hadn't gone anywhere yet!

'Perhaps,' she allowed, her pulse beating erratically at his close proximity, feeling that now familiar languor stealing over her as her thighs pressed intimately against his.

Cesare gave a knowing smile at the lack of

conviction in her tone. 'Maybe I should give you something to think about while I am gone…?' he suggested, and his head lowered and his mouth captured hers.

Robin kissed him back with all the pent-up emotion inside her, aching at the thought of his leaving and of the hollow loneliness she knew she was going to feel once he had gone…

'Robin, I— Perhaps the two of you *should* get married as soon as possible!' her father observed as they sprang guiltily apart to turn and look at him where he stood in the connecting doorway to his own office, next to Robin's. 'Or, alternatively, get a lock put on the door,' he amended, with wry acceptance of the inevitable. 'Correct me if I'm wrong, but didn't the two of you part only a couple of hours ago?'

Robin face burned with embarrassed colour at having her father find her and Cesare together like this twice in as many days. Although it did seem to have succeeded in convincing him of the intensity of their relationship…

'I'm sorry, Charles.' Cesare was the one to apologise, at the same time keeping his arm firmly about Robin's waist as he anchored her to his side. 'I have been called away on business suddenly, and wanted to see Robin before I left.'

'Of course,' her father agreed understandingly. 'I'll come back later—'

'That is not necessary,' Cesare assured the older man as he released Robin. 'I have to go now in any case. I will call you later, Robin.'

'Don't forget I'll be home a little late tonight if I'm going to the hotel to check on Catriona and Marco,' she reminded him, definitely intending to do just that. In fact, she was looking forward to it!

Cesare gave her a brief, searching look, before nodding abruptly to her and her father and leaving. A tense silence was left behind him.

'Catriona and Marco…?' Charles asked.

'Cesare's little nephew and his nursemaid live with Cesare,' Robin replied as she moved back to sit behind her desk, still a little embarrassed about her father walking in on her and Cesare in another compromising situation.

'Cesare's nephew? Is this nephew the heir you mentioned yesterday?' her father probed.

Robin gave him a wary glance. 'I thought I had told you Marco was Cesare's nephew…?' she prevaricated.

'No.' Her father spoke sharply. 'And this nephew lives with him, you say?'

'Yes…'

'How old is he?'

'About six months,' Robin answered slowly, uncertain where her father was going with this conversation. But he was certainly going somewhere…

'And Marco is the son of Cesare's late sister, Carla?' her father guessed.

'Yes, he is— Daddy, what's the problem?' Robin rejoined, her hands so tightly clenched beneath her desk that her nails were digging into her palms. Her father was far from stupid, and if he added two and two together… 'Cesare was left literally holding the baby when Carla…died.

And now he's adopted Marco as his own son,' she explained.

'Is this the reason you've agreed to marry him?' her father persisted.

Robin felt herself go pale, and was glad she was already sitting down—otherwise she might have fallen down. 'What do you mean?' she prompted weakly.

Her father crossed the room to look down at her searchingly.

'Robin, no one understood better than I did how you felt when you realised you would probably never have a child. But you can't marry a man just because he already has a baby for you to love as your own!' He looked perplexed. 'Darling—'

'Daddy, how can you even suggest such a thing after walking in on Cesare and I in the way you have during the last two days?' she cried with relief.

For one dreadful moment she really had thought her father had realised Cesare was blackmailing her into marriage by making her feel guilty about Carla's orphaned son!

Which would have been disasterous after all she had already done in order to keep the truth from him.

'Hmm, that's true,' her father accepted ruefully, after giving the idea some more thought. 'But the two of you falling in love in this way after…after what happened is a bit of a coincidence, you have to admit,' he added less certainly.

It was more than a coincidence—much more. But it was important that her father believed she was marrying Cesare because she loved him. And *only* because she loved him…

'I told you, Daddy, it was meant to be,' she assured her parent. 'And you're going to love Marco when you meet him. He's absolutely gorgeous.' She smiled dreamily.

'Looks like Gambrelli, does he?' her father asked, an eyebrow raised.

'He does actually, yes,' she came back brightly.

'Then this really is what you want, darling?' he asked.

'It's what I really want, Daddy,' she assured him firmly.

Her father gave her an indulgent smile back. 'In that case, it's good to see you happy again, Robin.'

Was she happy? Robin wondered, after her father had returned to his own office.

She was in love with a man who didn't love her, but who was going to marry her anyway and take her to his bed every night.

Take her to *their* bed every night, she corrected herself.

But Cesare wasn't going to have everything his own way in this marriage of theirs. No matter what he might think to the contrary....

Cesare stood very still and quiet in the doorway of Marco's nursery, held immobile by the scene before him.

The nursery night-light was switched on, but Marco was not in his cot as he should have been, at ten o'clock at night. Instead he lay asleep, cradled in the arms of Robin who sat in the bedroom chair, also asleep.

Marco was asleep in *Robin's* arms...!

It was so unexpected—the last thing Cesare had thought he would find after talking to her father on the phone and discovering Robin was still at the Gambrelli Hotel. He had been standing in the doorway of the nursery for the last five minutes, staring at the two of them.

Robin didn't particularly care about children. Her first husband had divorced her because she had delayed giving him the children he wanted. And yet here she was, cradling Marco so tenderly he might have been made out of porcelain.

Cesare didn't know what to make of it—had no idea how this could have come about.

His business in Nice concluded; he had decided to fly back to the UK tonight, instead of remaining until tomorrow morning in France.

But when he'd telephoned Robin's home, to tell her of his change of plan, her father had told him he believed her to still be at the Gambrelli Hotel.

Sure that it had to be impossible for Robin to still be there with Catriona and Marco, Cesare hadn't bothered to call and check. But his thoughts had been extremely dark during the flight back to London, as he'd wondered exactly what Robin was doing, still visiting the hotel.

Where his cousin Wolf was a guest, and might be also...

It was highly possible, Cesare had reasoned, that the two of them had met again accidentally while Robin was at the hotel. It was also highly feasible, knowing Wolf, that his cousin could have taken advantage of that accidental meeting to invite Robin to join him for dinner!

Except Wolf hadn't done any such thing. Because Robin had been here in Cesare's suite all the time—while he had been having such dark thoughts about her...

He didn't understand. Couldn't understand why Robin had remained here for the last three or four hours—let alone why she was in Marco's nursery, holding him as if she would never let him go!

He turned to leave, not wanting to wake either of them, and needing a drink after the trying day he'd had. Needing time and space too, to try and fathom out the mystery of Robin and Marco…

'Cesare?'

He turned at the sound of her voice, his expression closed as he raised dark brows.

Robin stared back at him, a sinking feeling in the pit of her stomach as she saw questions in Cesare's eyes.

Lots of questions.

And all of them had to be connected with finding her here in Marco's nursery, holding the small boy in her arms while he slept!

She avoided Cesare's probing stare to get carefully to her feet, without waking the baby. 'Just let me put Marco back in his cot and I'll be with you,' she told Cesare softly, and she walked over to the cot and laid the baby gently down, putting his teddy bear in beside him before covering them with the duvet. She straightened slowly. 'I sup-pose—'

'We will talk in the sitting room, Robin,' Cesare said quietly, holding the door open for her to leave.

Robin gave him a searching glance as she preceded him out of the room, quickly turning away as she saw the speculation in his eyes. She was not at all sure how she was going to explain herself out of this one!

'Brandy?' he offered abruptly, once they were in the sitting room, the door closed behind them so that they wouldn't be disturbed.

'Yes. Thank you,' she added, running the palms of her hands nervously down the skirt of her suit, having discarded her jacket some hours earlier when she'd got down on the floor to play with Marco.

It had been a wonderful evening as far as she was concerned, her time spent with this adorable child—eating her evening meal with him, and then bathing him before getting him ready for bed. Except she hadn't put him straight into his cot, but had once again held him in her arms until he'd fallen asleep on her shoulder, feeling so content and relaxed that she must have dropped off too.

Which was exactly where Cesare had found her!

'Thank you,' she said again as he handed her the glass of brandy.

'Er—your business meeting finished earlier than you expected, then?' She attempted to distract him from asking any questions about Marco.

Cesare took a large swallow of his own brandy before answering her. 'As you say, I concluded my business in Nice earlier than expected.'

He had flown to the south of France earlier today? To Nice? What was in Nice that he'd had to go there so urgently?

'What—?'

'Why—?'

They began speaking at once, both of them breaking off at the same time.

'You first,' Robin invited, before taking a sip of her own brandy. She had a feeling she was going to need it!

Instead of continuing to speak, Cesare looked at her for several long minutes, still totally mystified as to why Robin had been in Marco's nursery.

He had accused her of putting off having children. In truth, he had used it as a threat when he'd told her he intended for her to become Marco's mother as part of the settlement of this blood feud between their two families!

But she hadn't corrected him when he made his accusations.

Hadn't contradicted him, either, when he'd told her that he knew it was her selfishness that had caused her first husband to divorce her.

She had seemed to shy away from even touching Marco, as well, the night he'd introduced the two of them, giving him the impression that she was a little scared of babies.

But all those impressions were at complete odds with the look of extreme tenderness Cesare had seen on Robin's face as she'd placed Marco in his cot before gently covering him and his teddy bear with the duvet.

Something did not add up.

Not that it really mattered now.

Once he had confided in Robin what he had learnt in Nice today, he doubted she was going to feel that she owed him any explanations about anything!

In fact, Cesare very much doubted that she would ever want to see him again after tonight....

CHAPTER ELEVEN

'So…' Robin sat down in one of the armchairs as she addressed Cesare conversationally. 'What took you to Nice so urgently?'

'First, Robin,' Cesare drawled softly, 'I would like you to tell me what you were doing in Marco's nursery.'

Her gaze shifted slightly sideways as she wondered how best to answer him. The truth—that she already loved Marco and couldn't wait to become his mother—really wasn't something she wanted to share with Cesare.

She tried to sound unconcerned. 'Catriona had some phone calls to make, so I offered to put Marco to bed for her. Obviously it wasn't as easy as I had expected, but I guess I shall have to get used to it.'

Cesare watched her from across the room, his

expression unreadable. 'That is not really the truth, is it?' he finally commented gently.

Robin stiffened. 'I don't know what you mean. Surely you don't think I would ever do anything to harm—'

'No, of course I do not think that.' Cesare sighed as he strode forcefully across the room to stand in front of her. 'I have come to know you as a loyal sister. As a kind and caring daughter. A generous—a very generous—lover. I do not think you have it in you to intentionally harm anyone or anything.'

'Well, that's something I suppose,' Robin said wryly, before taking another sip of the warming brandy.

And she needed its warmth—felt a growing chill inside her as Cesare continued to probe remorselessly into the motives behind her unexpected behaviour towards Marco.

'It is more than something, Robin,' he pressed. 'Please tell me the real reason you offered to put Marco to bed.'

Robin blinked as sudden tears stung her eyes,

her breath catching in her throat as she tried to hold back her sadness and not totally betray herself.

'I already told you— Cesare?' she protested, as he reached out to take her glass of brandy from her, placing it on the coffee table with his own, before reaching out to gently grasp her arms and pull her to her feet.

He continued to hold her. 'Tell me why your husband divorced you,' he demanded.

'But you know—'

'I do not believe that I do.' He sighed again. 'I only know what your husband chose to tell me,' he explained. 'I want you to tell me the truth, Robin.'

Giles had been the one to tell Cesare he had divorced her because she'd tried to put off having his children? How could he have done that? How could he hurt her in that way after all she had already gone through in order to try and have the child they had so desperately wanted? After all the tests and examinations that had put such a strain on their marriage, without giving any real answer as to why she couldn't conceive, only that she hadn't? How could Giles have lied about all of that?

The tears fell unheeded down her cheeks now. 'Wouldn't it have been simpler for you to have asked me for the truth in the first place?' she protested emotionally.

Cesare released her to thrust his hands into his trouser pockets. 'Yes, it would,' he accepted heavily. 'But I— I'm asking you now, Robin,' he encouraged. 'Please?'

Robin stared at him, totally unsure of him in this mood. 'What happened in Nice, Cesare?' she asked warily.

Nice. Where Cesare's sister, Carla, had been having dinner with friends the night before she died...

Or was she just jumping to conclusions? Robin wondered frowningly.

Cesare's hands clenched into fists as he resisted the impulse to reach out and take Robin in his arms, and kiss her and keep on kissing her until this nightmare went away.

Except that he knew the truth now, and couldn't ignore it.

Even though it was a truth that would take Robin from him…

He had never even contemplated getting married before now, and this marriage to Robin was only supposed to have been the settlement of a blood feud. Except there was no longer anything to settle. Which meant he could no longer force Robin into marrying him.

Robin was going to walk out of his life tonight and never look back!

A reality that chilled his heart—the heart he had believed impervious…

His mouth tightened. 'I wish to talk about you first, Robin. Please tell me the truth. Did your marriage come to an end because you avoided getting pregnant?'

'No,' she answered tearily.

Cesare's breath left him in a long, shaky sigh. 'Then why did it end?' he continued gruffly.

Robin turned away as if she could no longer even bear to look at him. 'Because I couldn't give Giles the children he needed to carry on the Bennett line! I *couldn't* give him children, Cesare! There!' She turned to glare at him with glittering violet-coloured eyes. 'Are you happy now?' she challenged. 'I don't have children— will never have any children of my own—because despite months, years of trying, I just can't seem to become pregnant!' Her voice broke emotionally on that last word, and the tears once again began to fall down her creamy cheeks. 'I didn't want to tell you—didn't want you to know!' she choked.

Cesare stared at her as the full reality of what she had said hit him with the force of a punch slamming into his chest.

Robin couldn't have children…?

That body, that long, slender, perfect body that had been made to give and receive pleasure, could not carry the child of the man she loved? And Bennett had divorced her because of that?

Cesare wanted to punish something, someone, for the hurt and rejection Robin must have suffered at the hands of her selfish husband.

Robin's inability to have children did not make her less of a woman, so how could Bennett have done this to her?

But who was Cesare to criticise the other man when he had intended doing exactly the opposite—he hadn't given Robin's wants and needs a second thought, either, when he'd told her she would marry him and have his children!

Which made him no better than Giles Bennett…

How Robin must hate him. How she must hate both of them!

'I am so sorry, Robin…' he began.

The angry glitter in those purple eyes deepened. 'Keep your pity, Cesare!' she cried, going across the room to collect her jacket from where she must have draped it over a chair earlier. 'I need to leave now,' she added stiffly. 'We can continue this conversation tomorrow—'

'Sit down, Robin?' he requested. 'Sit,' he repeated softly, as she stared at him rebelliously.

She didn't want to sit down. She wanted to get out of here now—needed to go away somewhere and lick her wounds in private.

'Please, Robin,' Cesare persisted, standing so tall and remote across the room. 'I have to explain—have to tell you why I went to Nice today. You see, Robin, I owe it to you to tell you the truth.'

She drew in a deep, controlling breath, not really wanting to remain here and listen to him talking about Nice, but knowing that for her father's sake she should at least stay and hear what Cesare had to tell.

'Just answer me one question first, Cesare.' She spoke huskily.

'When you've finished telling me what you learnt in Nice today—' She broke off, swallowing hard, desperately trying to hold back further tears. 'Are you still going to demand that I marry you?' She faced him proudly, prepared for the blow she was sure was about to follow.

Cesare breathed harshly, his eyes shining darkly as he answered her. 'No,' he bit out. 'No, I will no longer have the right to demand anything from you, Robin,' he confirmed.

She hadn't been prepared for the blow at all,

Robin realised, and she staggered back to sit back down in the armchair, her face very pale as she stared up at him disbelievingly.

His mouth twisted self-deprecatingly. 'It would be a little more…flattering to me as a lover if you looked less relieved at the thought of escaping marriage to me!'

Relieved! Robin felt as if she'd had the floor kicked out from under her feet. As if all the air had been knocked out of her lungs. As if her world, her rosy world of the future that had contained Cesare and Marco, had been taken from her.

And it had…

Her lips felt numb, her tongue so dry she couldn't have spoken even if she had wanted to.

She wasn't going to be Cesare's wife.

Or Marco's mother.

Wasn't going to spend the rest of her life with the two people she already loved most in the world…

Her heart ached. She felt hollow inside. As if

all love, all emotion, had been taken from her in a single blow.

'I can see that this news is so welcome it has rendered you speechless with relief!' Cesare drawled, bending down to pick up his brandy glass and draining its contents in one swallow before moving to replenish it. He poured a double measure this time, sure that he was going to need it before this conversation was over.

In fact, once Robin had gone, he intended getting very drunk indeed!

He had been so wrong about her. He knew now that she hadn't made a conscious, calculated decision to delay having children at all, but instead had had that joy denied her and been totally rejected by her own husband because of it.

What had that done to her? How had that made her feel?

No wonder she had become known as the unnattainable Robin Ingram—she had been protecting herself from yet another rejection, not disdaining all relationships, as Cesare had assumed.

In fact, he now knew he had assumed rather too much altogether where Robin was concerned.

As well as seducing her into becoming his lover...

That was surely something he was going to have to live with for the rest of his life...

The memory of Robin in his arms alone was going to haunt him for the rest of his days—and nights!

He drew himself up, needing to get this over with, knew that Robin must want to get as far away from him as she possibly could. 'You remember that Wolf and I had breakfast together this morning...?'

This morning? his thoughts echoed heavily. Was it only this morning that he and Robin had lain in bed together after a night of lovemaking, on the point of passion yet again when Catriona had told them of the phone call that had been the start of this nightmare?

It seemed like much, much longer...

'Of course,' Robin confirmed flatly, very still

and pale now as she sat unmoving in the arm-chair.

Cesare nodded. Just looking at Robin now, at what he had done to her, was causing him pain. And it wasn't over yet…

'I had not seen Wolf since—since Carla's funeral.' He sighed. 'As I told you, we only met a few years ago, and we both lead busy lives—you understand? As a family we do not meet often.'

'Weddings and funerals?' Robin commented.

'Exactly,' Cesare agreed, remembering that he had not spoken to any of the other people who had attended Carla's funeral that bleak day, when he had been too devastated by his sister's death to even attempt polite conversation.

Perhaps if he had spoken to Wolf that day none of this—his vendetta against the Ingram family, his deliberately seeking Robin out and blackmailing her into marrying him—would have happened… He and Robin might even have met socially, perhaps at that charity dinner, might have come to know each other—

It was too late now for regrets! Too late now to

do anything but tell Robin the truth and then let her walk out of his life for ever...

Robin wished Cesare would get it over with— just tell her what he needed to say and then let her leave. Before she broke down completely.

'So—I had not seen Wolf since Carla's funeral,' he continued. 'We talked of Carla this morning, of course. He expressed his regrets, and he told me— Robin, he told me that he had seen Carla the night before she died.'

Robin gave a pained frown. 'You've already told me she was dining with friends in Nice that evening...'

'But that is the point, Robin,' Cesare went on heavily. 'Wolf told me that when he saw Carla she was dining with only one other person. A man. A man I now know to be Pierre Dupont!' he said harshly, his eyes flashing dangerously.

Robin blinked, trying to remember what Cesare had told her about that evening. 'But I thought you said Carla was dining with Pierre Dupont *and* his wife Charisse on the night she died...?'

'They lied!' he rasped angrily. 'The two of

them lied. The wife lied in order to protect her husband!' He began to pace the room. 'All during her pregnancy I tried to get Carla to tell me who was the father of her baby, but she always refused—insisted on protecting the name of her lover, assuring me that one day I would know, that once the baby was born everything would be all right. It was not. I realise now that Carla had always harboured the belief that once she had her lover's baby he would leave his wife and come to her.'

Robin's heart ached for the young-and-in-love Carla—for the dreams she must have had, the dreams that had surely been shattered...

Cesare grimaced. 'The night before the accident, Carla and Dupont met for dinner before going to her hotel room.' He shook his head. 'I cannot believe—' He drew in a deeply controlling breath. 'Afterwards, Dupont told Carla once and for all that he never intended leaving his wife—that he didn't want to see Carla again, let alone his son!'

'Oh, God...' Robin groaned, having already

suspected as much, but still unprepared for the callousness of Pierre Dupont.

'Carla was devastated. Distraught.' Cesare's eyes showed his anger at the pain and humiliation his sister had suffered. 'But nothing she could say made any difference to Dupont's resolve to remain with his wife, to end things between himself and Carla for ever. Robin, I know now that I was wrong, very wrong, when I told you that Carla was happy and relaxed when she drove out of Nice the morning of the accident. In reality she was as upset as your brother Simon was—maybe more so.'

Yes, Robin could believe that—could all too easily imagine Carla's pained disillusionment.

'She might even have been the one who caused the accident,' Cesare added quietly.

'We'll never know now.' Robin shook her head sadly.

'No,' he acknowledged heavily. 'But you do see how this changes things…?'

Oh, yes, she saw…

'What did you do to Pierre Dupont, Cesare?'

she asked suddenly, very aware of what he had tried to do to her own family—to her—in his quest for revenge for his sister's untimely death.

'I have done nothing to him,' he answered haughtily.

'Yet?' Robin guessed quietly.

'Yet,' he agreed. 'But that is not for you to worry about, Robin—'

'Having recently been on the receiving end of your anger, Cesare, I most certainly *do* worry about it!' she assured him hotly.

His mouth twisted humourlessly. 'A man like Dupont does not deserve your pity or your consideration!'

Cesare just didn't understand, did he? Didn't seem to realise that it wasn't Pierre Dupont she cared about, but Cesare himself, and what this senseless vendetta was doing to him. Couldn't he see that nothing he did or said now—to anyone—could ever bring Carla back to him?

'And what about you, Cesare?' she questioned hesitantly. 'Do you deserve my pity or my consideration?'

His eyes flickered with an emotion that he quickly masked. 'No,' he ground out. 'From you I deserve only contempt for what I have done to you. It is not enough for me to ask your forgiveness for the wrong I have done you and your family—'

'You could still ask, Cesare,' Robin told him softly.

He closed his eyes briefly, a nerve pulsing in the pallor of his tightly clenched jaw as he finally looked across at her. 'I would very much like your forgiveness, Robin,' he admitted raggedly.

'But there is nothing that I can do or say that will ever take away the wrong I have done your family, the hurt I have caused you—'

'You're forgiven, Cesare,' she cut in. 'Absolutely. Completely.' How on earth could she not forgive him when she loved him so much?

How on earth was she supposed to get up and just walk away when she loved him so much? And Marco…

He shook his head. 'It really cannot be that easy, Robin—'

'But it is, Cesare,' she assured him, once again picking up her jacket as she prepared to leave, knowing that it would do no good to prolong this agony. That it was over. All over. 'Why don't you try it some time, Cesare? It would certainly be better for you, and for everyone else, if you could learn a little forgiveness.'

'Dupont abandoned Carla when she most needed him,' Cesare persisted. 'Worse, with the help of his wife, he rejected both Carla and the son she had borne him—and then lied about it!'

Robin looked sympathetic. 'I appreciate that, Cesare, but vengeance is such a self-destructive emotion,' she warned sadly as she stood up. 'It will destroy you more than it destroys anyone else.'

'Is that how you see me?' He looked at her closely. 'As nothing more than a man of vengeance?'

'Of course it isn't,' she assured him, having no intention of telling him how she really viewed him. It was too late for that. 'But can't you see, Cesare? *You're* the one who will have the pleasure of bringing up Marco,' she reminded him. 'Of watching him grow into the fine young man I'm sure he's going to be—' She broke off as her voice broke emotionally, swallowing hard before continuing. 'Pierre Dupont will never know him—probably never see the son he rejected before he was even born. And isn't Marco's happiness what's really important?'

Cesare looked puzzled. 'You care for him…?'

'Yes,' she confirmed simply.

Because she would never have a son of her own, Cesare realised, with a pained wince at the things he had said and done to her, at the mistakes he had made where Robin was concerned.

Robin wasn't the cold, calculating woman he had accused her of being—he should have known that better than anyone after the way they had made love together! No, Robin was not in the least cold; her elusiveness where men were concerned had merely been an act of self-defence, so that she was never hurt again by any man's rejection.

'Marco could still be your son too, Robin,' he offered. 'You could still marry me...'

She gave a melancholy smile. 'I've already told you I don't want your pity, Cesare.'

It would not be pity! He wanted to marry Robin—wanted to be the one who protected her from any more hurt or pain!

He just didn't have the right—not after the things he had said and done—to ask that on his own behalf...

'I—we could start again?' he suggested gruffly. 'We could go out together, spend time together. You could spend time with Marco,' he added temptingly as he saw her shake her head.

'No, Cesare,' Robin answered firmly, more than ever determined that she would not accept Cesare's pity. His love, yes, but never his pity. And Cesare didn't love her— would never love her, no matter how much time they spent together. 'It would never work.'

'But—'

'No, Cesare!' she repeated tensely. 'I— It's better if we just end this now. We'll never know what happened in Monaco six months ago. All we do know is that we both lost beloved members of our family. Let's just leave it at that, shall we?'

'If that is what you wish,' he agreed reluctantly.

What she wished for she couldn't have!

'It is,' she confirmed briskly, desperate to get out of here now, not wanting to break down in front of Cesare a second time. 'But before I go I do need to know what you intend doing with the shares you own in Ingram Publishing—'

'They are yours,' Cesare assured her. 'You—'

'Don't you dare say I've earned them, Cesare,' Robin interrupted him angrily. 'Don't you *dare!*' she warned emotionally, knowing there was only one way in which she could have done that, and that night of lovemaking with Cesare was too precious to her to be belittled in that way.

He frowned darkly. 'I was not about to say that.'

'Weren't you?' she said disbelievingly.

'No!' Cesare came back. 'I have made many mistakes with you, Robin, and treated you in a way I am ashamed of. But I would never insult you in that way. Last night was…' He paused. 'I will never forget you, Robin.'

She would never forget him, either. How could she, when she loved him so much…?

'I was about to say that the shares in Ingram Publishing are yours to do with as you wish. I will have their transfer over to you witnessed first thing tomorrow morning, and then deliver them to you by special messenger.'

Once that had been done, Cesare acknowledged, it would mean that he had to break off all further contact with Robin.

Obviously Robin didn't share his reluctance for the impending severing of all contact between them.

And who could blame her? If he were in her place—if she had treated him as he had treated her—he would want to sever all contact between them too!

'Will you accept my word that that is what I will do?' he said.

'Of course, Cesare.' She smiled slightly. '*If*

nothing else, I know you to be a man of your word!'

If nothing else, he echoed hollowly.

'I wish you happiness for the future, Robin,' he told her sincerely.

'And I wish you the same, Cesare,' she returned, before turning sharply on her heel and walking away.

It was the hardest thing Cesare had ever done in his life to just stand by and let her...

CHAPTER TWELVE

'I SINCERELY HOPE you know what you're doing,' the man at Robin's side said, as he smiled and nodded his head in acknowledgement of the other guests attending the charity ball.

'Absolutely…not!' she replied happily, and she slipped her arm companionably into his. The room was heaving with the glitteringly rich and the dazzlingly beautiful.

'That's what I thought,' Count Wolf Gambrelli murmured ruefully, one of the glitteringly rich and dazzlingly handsome himself, in his black evening suit, snow-white shirt and red bow-tie. 'You do realise that you could be responsible for my dear cousin calling me out with pistols at dawn?'

'Doubtful,' Robin dismissed distractedly. Her attention was fixed on the huge double doors where the guests were being announced as they arrived. She wanted to be absolutely aware of when—if—Cesare made his entrance.

It had been three months since she'd seen Cesare. Three long, lonely months without him. But tonight, at this charity ball she had helped organise—significantly being held at the London Gambrelli Hotel—she hoped that she would at last see him again. He had accepted his invitation she had personally seen dispatched to him. But, as she knew only too well, Cesare had accepted the invitation to the last charity dinner she'd helped to organise, but had left before the actual meal.

There was always the chance that this time he might not put in an appearance at all!

'You could sound a little more concerned about my welfare, Robin,' Wolf reproved teasingly. 'I consider what we are doing akin to the barbaric sport of bear-baiting—and we all know what happened when the bear decided he had been baited long enough!'

'He mauled his tormentor to bits,' Robin agreed

unconcernedly, having come to know Wolf Gambrelli quite well since she had contacted him a week ago and invited him to be her partner this evening.

She hadn't wanted to involve her father in her plan to meet Cesare again. She knew that he was extremely defensive on her behalf where Cesare was concerned, if still a little bewildered at the sudden ending of their engagement.

Not surprisingly, since every time he had seen them together they hadn't seemed able to keep their hands off each other!

Wolf had no such illusions where his cousin was concerned, and had been more than willing to accompany her this evening. In fact, he was obviously enjoying the idea of stirring Cesare up a little.

'Exactly.' Wolf gave an exaggerated sigh. 'Perhaps it's as well that I have arranged to disappear later on this evening? You do realise, I hope, that I would not be assisting you at all if it wasn't for the fact that I am tired of watching my poor cousin rage about Europe, dispensing woe and misery on all those unfortunate enough—like myself—to agree to have dinner with him!'

'Don't try and fool me, Wolf.' Robin chuckled appreciatively, knowing that his lazy humour hid a brain as sharp and decisive as his cousin's. 'I know how much you've been looking forward to witnessing this confrontation between Cesare and myself.' She chewed worriedly on her bottom lip, not at all as confident as she wanted to appear.

Not as confident as she wanted to *be!* She simply had no idea how Cesare was going to react to seeing her again—with or without his cousin Wolf at her side!—but she needed to see him. And other than making an appointment—something she had no intention of doing—this was the only way she had been able to think of to attract his attention. Good or bad.

'You—'

'Signor Cesare Gambrelli,' the page at the door announced clearly.

'He's here!' Robin's fingers tightened about Wolf's arm.

'Well, of course he's here, Robin,' he soothed. 'It only now remains for him to challenge me to those pistols at dawn!'

'It could be swords,' Robin muttered, as she searched through the crowd for that first longed-for glimpse in three months of the man she loved.

'How comforting!' Wolf murmured ruefully.

Not comforting at all, Robin acknowledged, as her tension rose to such a pitch that she was trembling. What if Cesare saw her and didn't even speak to her? What if he saw her with Wolf but decided only to speak to his cousin? What if—?

'Robin.'

Her fingernails dug painfully into Wolf's arm as she realised that while she had been so anxiously watching for Cesare across the crowded room he must have skirted around the side of the room and now stood behind her.

She looked beautiful, Cesare thought as Robin turned to face him. Even more so than when he'd last seen her three months ago, if that were possible. And it shouldn't have been, because even then he had known her to be the most beautiful creature alive.

But now she absolutely radiated beauty— seemed filled with an inner glow that made her eyes sparkle, her complexion glow, and her hair shine as it cascaded loosely about her bare shoulders. She was in a gold dress that hinted at rather than hugged the curves of her body, and she was happy, Cesare recognised heavily. Happier than he had ever seen her.

He turned a tight smile on his cousin. 'Wolf,' he greeted flatly.

'Cesare,' Wolf drawled smoothly. 'That's it— bear-baiting over,' he whispered in Robin's ear, before taking hold of the arm she had linked with his and placing it firmly in the crook of Cesare's. 'I think I deserve to be best man at the wedding after this!' he added mischievously, before departing.

Cesare frowned down at Robin, not understanding his cousin's teasing remark, only really aware of the fact that Robin hadn't removed her arm from where Wolf had placed it on his...

He was also aware of her elusive perfume, her warmth, and did not want this moment of closeness to end just yet. 'Would you care to dance?' he invited formally.

She smiled slightly. 'The dancing doesn't come until after the meal, Cesare,' she told him quietly.

'I am aware of that. But there is music.' A small orchestra played in one corner of the room. 'We have room to dance here.' He indicated the space that had emerged around them. 'And I would very much like to dance with you, Robin.'

Everyone would think them mad, Robin realised. Ridiculous, even. But did she really care?

'Yes, please,' she accepted softly, moving confidently into his arms, and inwardly sighing with pleasure when she felt his hand upon the small of her back as he drew her close to him. They began to move slowly in time to the music.

She could have stayed like that all evening, secure in Cesare's arms, but as the music played, and they continued to dance—neither of them aware of the curious looks being sent their way or the speculative comments—Robin knew that they would eventually have to make some sort of conversation.

'If you want to know why Wolf was here—'

'I do not.' Cesare stopped her. 'I decided three months ago never to jump to any assumptions where you are concerned ever again.'

She looked at him curiously. 'You did…?'

'Yes,' he assured with a rueful smile. 'Look what happened the last time I did that!'

She nodded. 'You almost married me.'

Almost. So close. He had come so close to having this delightful creature as his wife. For all the wrong reasons, of course. But that could have changed after a time— *would* have changed! Instead he had made Robin hate him.

'How is your father?' he enquired politely.

'Oh, Daddy is very well,' she answered happily. 'And Marco? How is he?'

'Crawling,' Cesare responded. 'It takes me all of my time to keep up with him now.' He paused. 'You are still working at Ingram Publishing?'

'For the moment,' she replied, suddenly seeming to avoid the darkness of his gaze.

'For the moment…?' Cesare repeated slowly, remembering all too clearly how absolutely adamant Robin had been that she would continue to work with her father after the two of them were married. What had happened to change her mind about that?

Or perhaps he should wonder who…?

Robin wasn't sure that this crowded room was the best place to tell Cesare her news. But, conversely, she wasn't sure she would ever have another opportunity to tell him, either!

'I only intend working for another four months or so,' she explained. 'Then I shall be taking maternity leave.'

She raised her head to look directly into his eyes as she made this last announcement.

Giving her every opportunity to see Cesare's reaction to what she had just said—the initial surprise, followed by shock, followed by another emotion that she couldn't read as those dark eyes blazed down at her fiercely.

'Robin…?' Cesare finally managed to gasp disbelievingly. 'But I thought you weren't able to have children...'

'So did I,' she dismissed with a happy smile. 'But obviously it isn't true.'

'Robin, are you telling me—? Are you—? Is it—?'

'I am. I am again. And, yes, it is.' She huskily confirmed what he didn't seem able to ask. 'In six months' time I am going to have our baby.' Her voice broke emotionally even as she smiled with happiness. 'After all my problems in the past I've had to have tests and things, but I've success-fully passed the twelve-week mark and— Cesare, what are you doing?' She laughed protestingly as he took a firm hold on her arm and began to stride forcefully through the crowd.

A crowd that seemed to part in front of them, as if aware of the drama that was being played out before them.

Though the show was soon over, as Cesare took her into his private lift, closing the doors firmly behind them before pressing the button for the top floor.

He looked down at her dazedly. 'I do not know what to say…' he finally murmured softly.

Robin felt her smile slip slightly. But only slightly. Because whatever happened she was going to have Cesare's baby.

It was a miracle. An undreamt-of miracle. One that Robin still had trouble believing, pinching herself when she woke each morning just to make sure that it wasn't a dream.

And it wasn't. Her consultant—the same consultant she'd had during her marriage to Giles—had been as surprised as she when she'd gone to his clinic six weeks ago and he had confirmed the suspicion she'd had that she was pregnant.

None of the tests she'd undergone years ago had ever been able to confirm the reason why she hadn't become pregnant during her marriage to Giles, only that she hadn't, and so Robin had just accepted that she would never have children of her own.

But that one night with Cesare, with the two of them making love together, had changed all that.

She really was pregnant. With Cesare's child.

Which was the reason she'd had to see him to-night. Why she'd had to talk to him. Had to at least tell him he was to become a father.

'You don't have to say anything, Cesare,' she assured him warmly. 'I just thought you had a right to know, that's all.'

'That is all? Robin, do you have any idea—' He broke off as the lift doors opened onto the penthouse suite.

'Do you have Marco with you?' she asked excitedly as she stepped out into the hallway.

'Of course,' he confirmed. 'But—'

'Could I see him?' Robin asked longingly.

'But of course.' Cesare frowned. 'I very much doubt that he is in bed just yet. But—'

'Oh, do let's go and see him before he goes to bed,' Robin encouraged eagerly. She was longing to see the little boy again—but also delaying the moment when Cesare would tell her how he felt about her being pregnant with his baby.

After all, he had made no effort to see her again after they'd parted three months ago. And it was only the need she'd felt to tell him of her pregnancy that had given her the courage to seek him out now.

There was always the chance that it would mean nothing to him at all…

Cesare stood back and watched Robin as she sat down on the nursery floor to play with Marco with complete disregard for the designer label gown she wore. She was only concerned with Marco—with making him laugh and chuckle as she picked him up in her arms and blew teasingly against his neck, laughing herself as the fact that he was teething made him dribble down her gown.

Cesare knew the reason for Robin's inner glow now—the reason she looked so happy. She was expecting the baby she had thought for ever denied her.

His baby!

He had gone to hell and not returned these last three months since parting from Robin—could hardly believe she was here now, let alone that she was expecting their child.

A child they had made during that one memorable night together.

'Don't frown so, Cesare,' Robin chided as she looked across the nursery at him, with Marco still held securely in her arms. 'I'm not expecting anything from you, you know. I just thought you should know about your baby.'

Not expecting—!

'Robin.' He moved to sit on the floor beside her, taking Marco from her arms to place him between them on the carpet. 'I am…overwhelmed by your news—'

'Well, of course you are,' she accepted lightly. 'I was overwhelmed to start with too. But now I'm just…happy.' She laughed.

Cesare reached out to cradle the side of her face with his hand, looking deeply into her eyes, those deep purple eyes that had haunted his dreams for months. 'You are so beautiful, Robin,' he breathed, his heart beating erratically in his chest. 'So very, very beautiful. I cannot tell you— Robin, I love you,' he told her intensely. 'I love you so much that it is impossible to express it in words!'

Robin stared at him—barely breathing, not moving, totally unable to believe what he was saying to her.

'You— You love me?' she finally managed chokingly. 'Because of the baby?'

'Not just because of the baby,' he assured her firmly. 'I loved you three months ago, when there was no baby! But I had to let you go—had already hurt you so much… Robin, I love you more than life itself. More than anything or anyone else. These last three months without you have been—' He broke off, shaking his head. 'I cannot begin to tell you how I have missed you, how I have longed for you, what torture my life has been without even a glimpse of you—'

'You loved me three months ago?' Robin finally managed to gasp as she stared at him disbelievingly.

His mouth softened. 'I know how difficult that must be for you to believe after the way I behaved—but, yes, I loved you then. It was because

I loved you that I had to let you go.' He groaned at the memory. 'I had hurt you enough with my vendetta, and I deserved to lose you. But can you not give me another chance now, Robin?' he pressed intently. 'Can you not find it in that generous heart of yours to give me the chance, the opportunity, to show you how much I love you—how much I want to marry you and be with you for ever?'

'But…but…I can't—' Robin was totally thrown—couldn't believe that Cesare was actually telling her he had loved her all those months ago…!

'You cannot forgive me for the way I behaved,' he acknowledged heavily, turning away. 'And why should you?' he added bitterly as he stood up. 'I do not deserve a second chance. Do not deserve you! I will leave you now. Please stay with Marco as long as you wish,' he invited huskily, before turning away.

Robin paused only long enough to place Marco in his cot with several of his toys before hurrying after Cesare, no longer stunned by his admission of love for her but burning to tell him that she felt the same way about him.

All the time they had wasted!

'What— What are you doing, Robin?' Cesare gasped as he reached the sitting room and she launched herself into his arms.

'I love you, Cesare,' she cried ecstatically as she showered his face with kisses. 'I love you, I love you, I love you!'

'You— Dear God,' he cried, and his arms moved about her waist to pull her tightly against him as he buried his face in the scented silk of her hair. 'You love me? You really love me, Robin?'

'For months and months,' she admitted, as she nibbled on his earlobe.

'Months? You loved me three months ago too!' he realised. 'But if that is so why would you not give me another chance, Robin? Why—'

'Because I didn't know that you loved me. It seemed that your offer came out of pity—'

'The only person I pitied was myself—for having been so stupid, so arrogant, so unforgiving—'

'Hey, you're talking about the man I love!' she cut in teasingly.

Cesare could hardly believe this was happening after all the months of being without her. 'I thought about what you said, and I took your advice about Pierre Dupont,' he told her. 'You were right. It is punishment enough that he will never know the joy that is Marco.'

'I'm glad, Cesare,' she reached up to touch his cheek tenderly. 'For your sake, I'm glad.'

'I never intend for you to doubt my love ever again, Robin,' he vowed as he kissed her eyes, her nose, the soft pout of her lips. 'I want to be with you for ever!'

'And I with you!' she assured him glowingly. 'For ever and ever, Cesare!'

'Marry me?' he urged. 'Please marry me, Robin!'

'Oh, yes,' she breathed with certainty. 'Yes, yes, *yes!*'

Cesare looked down at her searchingly. 'Is it safe for us to make love? If not, I would just like to take you to bed and hold you. Hold you and never let you go,' he admitted raggedly.

'It's safe, Cesare.' Robin smiled up at him, love shining in her eyes as he swung her up into his arms to carry her into the bedroom and lay her tenderly down on the bed before joining her there. She put her arms up about his shoulders to pull him close. 'I love you, Cesare Gambrelli. I'll always love you,' she vowed.

'As I will always love you,' he assured her fiercely, before his head lowered and his mouth claimed hers.

Heaven.

EPILOGUE

'MARCO WILL BE beside himself with joy at having another sister,' Cesare told Robin, as he kissed the knuckles of her hand, which he held so tightly in his—the hand he had held all the way through Robin's labour and the birth, only minutes ago, of their third daughter.

'Three daughters in four years, Cesare.' Robin laughed happily, a little tired from the delivery, but longing for them to finish cleaning and swaddling her new daughter so that she might hold her in her arms again, having held her only briefly after her arrival. 'Never mind Marco's happiness, Cesare—how will you ever cope once our daughters are all grown up and looking for husbands of their own?' she teased, knowing that her husband absolutely adored all of their children: Marco, Carla, Simone, and now their adorable Anna.

'Wolf has suggested I buy a gun to keep their suitors at bay,' he drawled wryly. 'Personally, I had thought of installing an electrified fence!'

Robin chuckled. 'I'm sure that between you, and Marco—along with their grandfather, of course—will manage quite adequately without the gun or the electrified fence!'

Cesare sobered, his gaze fierce as he looked at her. 'I love you so much, Robin. The years I have spent with you have been the happiest of my life. You *are* my life!'

'As you are mine,' she assured him, that same love glowing in her eyes.

Their marriage had been four years of joy and happiness, of growing closer together, their love having strengthened and deepened until they couldn't bear to be apart, even for a short time.

It was a love that they both knew would never end.

* * * * *